travels with marie

Hey Neil -
I like your name so
much I gave it to the
husband of my main
character - crazy huh? :)
I'm so grateful for your
friendship! Lucky me -
Wish you all the best
of everything!
Hugs + thanks,
Barb

the magical life...

travels with marie

our island adventure

BARB E. CALL

TATE PUBLISHING & *Enterprises*

Published by Tate Publishing & Enterprises, LLC
127 E. Trade Center Terrace | Mustang, Oklahoma 73064 USA
1.888.361.9473 | www.tatepublishing.com

Tate Publishing is committed to excellence in the publishing industry. The company reflects the philosophy established by the founders, based on Psalm 68:11,
"The Lord gave the word and great was the company of those who published it."

Cover design by Lance Waldrop
Interior design by Sarah Kirchen

Published in the United States of America

ISBN: 978-1-61777-591-8
1. Fiction / Contemporary Women
2. Fiction / Humorous
11.09.14

ACKNOWLEDGMENTS

To my dear friend Marie, who lights up a room with her smile, and my four wonderful sisters, who are my favorite traveling companions: Jan, Maudie, Margie, and Ruth, who have provided me wonderful memories and more than enough material to create this island adventure.

TABLE OF CONTENTS

THE ADVENTURE BEGINS

Sam and Melanie Walker moved their family from Boulder, Colorado to Wheaton, Maryland the year I entered the third grade. Luckily for me, the Walkers had a daughter who was just my age, named Marie. Marie was a petite, dark-headed beauty with big, blue eyes and lips that curved up in a pretty way. We became inseparable.

You could say Marie and I grew up together in Wheaton, Maryland. Since Marie's last name was Walker and mine was Wells, we were always seated next to each other every year at school through elementary and junior high, but when it was time to enter high school, we were forced to separate. I enrolled at Wheaton High, but Marie's parents insisted that she attend the newly built Blessed Mary Sacred Heart Catholic school. Marie begged me to convert and join the Catholic church so we could attend Blessed Mary Sacred Heart together, and I did accompany her to Mass on three separate occasions, but the Catholic church was cavernous, drafty, and, for lack of a better word, creepy. I couldn't understand a word spoken by the stern-looking Priest who was in charge there. He wore strange hats and had a high, nasal sounding voice. He had thick bushy eyebrows and beady black eyes that seemed to go in two differenct directions at the same time. I suspected him of being able to see right into the minds of any who fell under his piercing gaze. If this were true, and I strongly suspected it was, I was sure the moment one of his eyes found me, he would immediately stop in the middle of his Latin condesension, or whatever it was called, force me to stand and approach his holy padded bench and publicly consign me to hell for my thoughts about our school football captain, Josh Halltree, making passionate love to me in the back of his El Camino.

The nuns at that place weren't any better. They were super strict and they made Marie wear a hideous brown uniform which was anything but fashion forward... but then, I don't think nuns really care all that much about fashion. I could never understand why any young girl in her right mind would sign up to wear those depressing, completely non-flattering black robes, lace-up shoes, weird cardboard forehead strips and white stretchy neck wraps for the rest of their lives. No wonder the nuns at Marie's church all looked so serious and depressed. I couldn't see Marie having much fun at that school and, truth to tell, neither could Marie, which is why she turned into a juvenile delinquent during her sophomore year in order to get kicked out, which happened the moment she got caught after organizing and running a nearly successful panty raid on the Nuns private quarters. Marie's head was hung in shame, but a sly little smile played on her lips as Sister Euphemia briskly marched her right off the school property. The next week I made Dustin Wanker, who had a distinct foot odor problem, move to another seat so Marie could sit next to me in homeroom at Wheaton High. We were back on track.

During our senior year, tragedy struck. Marie's family moved to Pennsylvania, home of Penn State. Her dad was relocated there to be head of some big corporation. Marie was furious, dug in her heels and refused to go. I was pretty unhappy about the development myself. Marie and I concocted a plan and informed our parents we were quitting school, getting jobs and moving in together. Two days later, Marie waved a sad good-bye from the back seat of her parents' station wagon. In the following months we spent all our babysitting money calling each other long distance, during which we planned our future together. Marie had no problem convincing me to join her the following year at Penn State. We applied and were both accepted. We studied all the majors and decided to go into Interior Design. It looked like a relatively easy major, affording us plenty of time for our true vocations, which were shopping at the mall, skiing, researching popular fashion trends, doing our make-up and hair… oh, and flirting with boys. Another key reason for our decision to become interior designers was because the decorators who designed her parents' new house made a bundle of money and all they did was turn the whole place brown, purple, and a heinous color called okra. Marie's parents, who were evidently color blind, loved it.

We planned to revolutionize the interior design industry with a distressed look we came up with and which we referred to *shabby sheik,* and which, later on, after we'd abandoned the idea completely, became some other designer's billion dollar business model. It was that way with all our clever ideas and innovative inventions—somebody *else* always turned them into reality and got very rich later on.

LOVE AND MARRIAGE

Marie and I didn't actually experience the magical social life we had so carefully planned the summer before we entered college. We flirted a lot, dated creeps and losers almost exclusively, and watched our classmates fall in love with the non-creeps and losers, and get married in big, beautiful fairy-tale weddings with annoying regularity, while we stood around in whatever hideous bridesmaid dresses had been selected for the occasion. We finally decided at the ripe old age of twenty, that true love was a myth, and who wanted a couple sex-crazed Neanderthals draped over our bodies trying to grope us the minute the lights went out anyway? Well... Marie and I began looking more favorably upon the virtues of a really good grope.

But then, in our third year of school, something wonderful happened. It was a Saturday morning. We were going through some design layouts in the front room of the place we were renting, when we noticed a red convertible pull up right in front of the house. A tall, nice looking young man unfolded himself from the tiny car and stood there on the street, looking up at the house. From the way he was dressed, it was clear he was a student. He was outfitted in loafers, khaki slacks, a button down shirt and casual sport coat. A pair of sunglasses completed the look. To our utter amazement and joy he walked right up to the front door and rang the bell. Marie catapulted across the room and opened the door. Mr. big and tall, standing there in his cool sunglasses smiled down at her, introduced himself as Jack Davies, and asked if the house still had a room to rent. Marie started to offer *her* room, but I stepped in and asked if he was sure he had the right house, since only girls lived in this one. There was another house looking for male student renters, but it was across the street and several blocks away. He looked down at a paper he was holding in his hand, stepped back to study the numbers on the house and appeared to have an "ah ha" moment. He told us he was just transferring from another school, didn't know the area, and apologized. Marie fell all over herself explaining how easily one could make a mistake like that since the numbers on our house and the one he was seeking were a combination of the same numbers and would he like to come in for cookies (which we didn't have) and a glass of lemonade, (another fantasy food item we did not possess) and allow her to enlighten him about the area and weekend student activities? She turned on the worst Rita Hayworth imitation I'd ever seen, but it seemed to work. He took off his glasses, revealing beautiful hazel eyes and accepted her invitation with a wide 'aw shucks maam' country boy smile and.... I'm not sure but I think he actually blushed. Geeze, did this guy just fall off the potato truck or what? Marie fed him Pepsi and Ho Hos, which, like any normal all-American college boy, he gobbled down with gusto. Marie and Jack struck up a friendship while getting high on sugar. Before departing that day, Jack invited Marie to some art exhibit on campus. She accepted, and that was it. Jack and Marie became a "couple."

One evening Jack showed up with one of his roommates, to provide a fourth for an evening of cards. His roommate's name was Neil Taylor and from the moment he walked in, I was smitten. Unfortunately, the handsome Mr. Taylor was less smitten with me. Neil was nice enough, but he seemed quiet, reserved, and preoccupied. My bubbly, vivacious personality and low-cut blouse seemed to have no effect on him whatsoever, and when the evening was over it appeared our non-budding relationship was over, too.

Months passed and I was left at home, working on design projects by myself while Marie and Jack sailed through one thrilling date after another.

Just as I was about to die of boredom, loneliness and jealousy, our seldom-ever-there roommate named Violet Katz, organized an auction for the purpose of raising funds for some worthy cause she had become passionate about, and Marie and I were prevailed upon to create an attractive "prize" involving us and domestic talents we did not possess, which a bunch of guys would be anxious to bid a lot of money for. Marie declined on the grounds that Jack wouldn't like her doing service projects for any other guys. So, that left me. I came up with a "one month service bundle" for some lucky guy, which included numerous plates of homemade cookies, a weekly car wash, one oil change (my brothers had actually taught me how to do this,) doing the guy's laundry for one month.... or maybe *twice,* and typing either one big paper or three smaller class assignments.

My service "bundle" received more bids than any other prize offered, and Violet was thrilled. The morning after the auction I received a call from the guy who had bid the most and won my prize. His name was Neil something. Twenty minutes later Neil showed up on our doorstep with a laundry basket full of clothes. Suddenly it hit me. This was him.... Jack's roommate, Neil Taylor. Oh great. A guy I had really been attracted to who had only been disinterested and bored by me. But Neil was not bored or disinterested today. Today Neil was gracious and friendly. He smiled over the laundry basket and said, "Hey, I know you! You're Kay Wells. Do you remember me? Long time no see, huh?" I pulled the basket out of his arms and responded with a curt, "Yep, Kay Wells—that's me. I'll return your laundry later this afternoon. Maybe you could write up a schedule of times for delivery of the other services I offered and have that ready when I come, okay? Thanks." I started to close the door, but he stepped firmly inside the doorframe.

"Hey Kay, hold on! Is something wrong? Have I said something to put you off?" Was this guy kidding? I offered my friendliest smile.

"No Neil, not at all. I'm sorry if I seemed a little short with you just now, but I have a lot to do today!" I inclined my head toward the laundry basket and continued,-"Honestly, you're fine. And, thanks for doing the auction. The money we raised will help a lot of people." Neil's expression relaxed again into an easy smile and he stepped back. "Well, I think I got the best prize. Guess I'll see you later this afternoon then. I'll be studying at the library for awhile, but I'll be home after three, okay?" I smiled, nodded, and gently closed the door.

It wasn't until three weeks later after delivering my umpteenth plate of chocolate chip cookies, that Neil shared with me why our first encounter had not been all that congenial. He'd just learned his mother had been diagnosed with cancer the day before our first "date," and his mind was not on the card game that evening, but he owed Jack a favor and said "O.K." to the date. The doctors performed surgery on Neil's mom, and were able to remove a tumor along with a few suspicious looking lymph nodes. A couple months of radiation treatments later and Neil's mom was back to her normal routine, free and clear of cancer. I felt my icy heart melt toward Neil Taylor that day, and I turned from businesslike service rep for the cause in jeans and baggy sweatshirts, to flirty "girl next door" in make-up, cute skirts and form-fitting tops. Neil had been flirting with me for some time before I let down my guard, so after that we quickly became an item. Three months into our whirlwind romance, Neil proposed.

That summer, in June, Neil and I married. Jack and Marie stood with us as best man and Maid of honor. The following month we performed the same services for them.

Jack and Neil started an internet software company. This was at a time when computer technology had just sprung to life, and their fledgling company took off. We mortgaged homes right across from each other on the same leafy, tree-lined street in the suburb of Brookhaven, Pennsylvania, and eagerly embarked upon married life.

Marie and I didn't miss a beat. We chatted on the phone or visited each other nearly every day. As couples, we enjoyed frequent evenings out and took family vacations together. Neil and Jack experienced ups and downs in their business. Fortunately, they enjoyed more ups than downs. We were never going to be rich, but we all lived comfortably.

Neil and I welcomed our first child, Megan Marie, nine months after saying "I do," and Ted was born a year after that. Then came little Suzi.

Marie and Jack had Jake, then Sam, and Bethanie Kay was born eleven months later. Marie was not happy with Jack over that little "surprise," but Beth was a pure delight.

The years flew by, full of soccer games, PTA meetings, dance recitals, driver's ed, ACT's, first crushes and family dinners. Suddenly, or so it seemed, our children were grown and we'd arrived at our 23rd wedding anniversaries.

Marie and I would never forget every detail of that day. We had just sent Suzi and Beth off to university and were all finally in the position of being "empty nesters."

The original plan for our "big twenty-third" was to have a backyard barbeque and enjoy our first "empty nester" anniversary quietly relaxing at home, but at the last minute, Jack and Neil decided to surprise us. Marie and I would, throughout the rest of our lives, be deeply grateful to our husbands for their inspired decision to make our twenty-third anniversary one of the most memorable and special of all.

Jack and Neil were up early that morning, loading our white minivan for a day trip. Marie and I loved day trips so when our husbands planned a twenty-third anniversary getaway for us, we were thrilled. I bagged up some cinnamon rolls; Marie brought some bottled water and fresh fruit and we headed north.

The sun was just creeping over the horizon as we drove to one of our favorite places in all the world… well, in all of Pennsylvania, that is. We'd never *seen* much else of the world, but still, anyone who has not visited Kennett Square and strolled through the Dupont Estates, more familiarly known as Longwood Gardens, has missed the opportunity to see a perfect re-creation of the Garden of Eden. Neil swung into the Longwood Gardens parking lot, and we made our way through the entrance.

Being the first of June, the gardens were dressed for summer. Exquisite flowers were everywhere, in banks and borders, bowers and clusters. Numerous varieties of trees lovingly planted throughout the grounds stood towering and majestic. The architecture, houses, and conservatories were simply… magnificent. The grassy areas were a shimmering sea of green, and the paths leading off the sidewalks into shaded glades and woodlands were scintillating and beaconing. The day was perfect. The waterfalls sparkled and danced. The lakes on the property were, predictably, home to mommy and daddy swans and ducks with their little ones in tow. We walked through the conservatories, feasting our eyes upon exotic plants and trees typically grown in the tropical rainforests of South America. We sat contentedly on the grass while enjoying the magnificent lily ponds in their quiet splendor. We walked through the original Dupont estate home and lunched on one of the porches of a second mansion, which had been converted to a grand restaurant.

We walked until we were tired and rested with ice cream cones on one of the many small benches, strategically placed everywhere. A group of wandering minstrels straight out of sixteenth century England strolled through the grounds singing madrigals most of the morning, which was delightful. Strangely, they just seemed to belong there too. It was a magical place, frozen in time and yet, ever-changing.

I always wondered where the mountain of gardeners and groundskeepers for this place were, and exactly when it was they worked on the property to keep it so pristine and perfect all the time. I concluded they must do all their gardening at night, like elves, but how could they see what they were doing in the dark? Unless all the groundskeepers wore night-vision goggles, or maybe they lighted the whole place up at night with big spot-lights just for the gardeners and grounds people to do their work. It was another mystery.

As the shadows lengthened and darkness began to settle over us, we made our way to the big fountains on the property and found a seat in the viewing area. There was always a colorful nighttime fountain display set to music, providing an ideal ending to our divine day in the gardens. We donned sweaters and jackets as the sun set. Cool evening breezes, brimming with the heartwarmingly familiar, earthy scents of summer filled our senses. It was heaven. After the fountain display, we toasted each other with cups of hot cocoa, and then we made our way to the car and traveled back home.

TRAGEDY AND NEW BEGINNINGS

Some men live for Super Bowl Sunday. They seem to worship football. Our husbands were like that about duck hunting. They never missed the first day of hunting season. They talked about it for weeks and planned their hunting trips down to the last detail.

The months following our 23rd anniversaries turned unseasonably cold, and the icy winds of winter moved in right before hunting season was scheduled to begin. On the morning Jack and Neil left for their hunting trip, the skies were gray and there was ice on the roads, but the TV weather forecaster spoke of clearing skies and warmer weather ahead. Neil and Jack drove confidently out of the city and headed up into higher elevations where the lakes and ducks awaited their arrival. Suddenly, a man driving a semi-tractor trailer lost control, careened around the bend of a narrow mountain road, and skidded directly into the path of Jack's little Chevy pickup. Our husbands were both killed instantly. Devastation, pain, loss and confusion followed.

An investigation of the accident revealed the trucking company had sent the truck out with faulty brakes, so both Marie and I received a settlement. The settlements, along with the generous life insurance policies our husbands carried, enabled us to pay off our homes and debts, with a respectable amount left over to live on. But money could not replace the husbands we loved, needed, and cherished, especially when their leaving was sudden and unforeseen.

Upon receiving the tragic news, our extended families and grown children rushed home from locations all across the country to help with funeral arrangements and to receive and give support and comfort. Our children stayed with us as long as they could, but their own lives could be put on hold only so long. Eventually, one by one, they returned to their homes, businesses, and for Sam, Suzi, and Beth, back to university.

Marie shut herself in her house and watched the cooking channel on television, all the while taking copious notes. Then, she turned into a maniac chef and spent hours either in her kitchen or in mine, re-creating all the dishes she'd observed on TV. Both our kitchens became cluttered with the most modern cookery accoutrements imaginable.

Unfortunately, Marie's newly developed joy of cooking combined with our stress-induced, out of control eating caused a sharp increase in our need for larger pants, adding even more grief to our already loaded weekly sessions of grief therapy.

Like Marie, I also spent a lot of time in front of the television, only I was drawn to the home shopping network. I sat and sobbed as pretty girls modeled anniversary rings for mom and displayed neat gadgets and gifts for dad. I sucked down bottles of Yoo-hoo and snacked on ding dongs and ice cream while ordering a large number of items from QVC that I didn't need. Then, I wrapped everything up and took it all over to Marie's.

A little over a year later, Marie and I let go of our grief. We finally realized we were wasting our lives shlumping around in old, oversized Lake of the Ozarks T-shirts and baggy sweatpants, ordering more and more junk we didn't need. Our grown children became worried over our constant depression, lack of energy, and apparent determination to eat ourselves into a carnival side-show exhibit, and to television-shop ourselves into insolvency. They were on the verge of having us packed off to The Home at Trembling Hills for the terminally unstable, when we finally said, "All right, *enough.*"

We dragged ourselves to the mall, bought the most attractive clothes we could find in our new, *larger* sizes and started going out to places like the library and local museums, to plays, and the symphony. We would drive to the mall and stride purposefully around for a while, calling it "exercise," as we window-shopped and browsed through racks of clothes. We knew we weren't really working out all that hard since we always used the escalator rather than the stairs and made regular stops at the food court. One afternoon, we were sitting in a little coffee shop, sipping strawberry cream Frappuccinos (low fat), while re-discussing the pros and cons of joining Weight Watchers, when we noticed a tall, fashionably dressed woman with fiery red hair, in huge sunglasses and an enormous hat. She was standing at the cash register, paying for a bag of raspberry scones. The woman exuded an air of confidence. When she spoke, we recognized an unmistakable New England accent. And then she laughed. It was that same musical laugh we'd heard so often at college. Both Marie and I stared at her, then at each other.

Marie leaned toward me and whispered, "Can you believe it? It's Violet Katz!" I nodded vigorously, my eyes wide.

"Oh my gosh, Marie, you're right! It *is* Violet! Should we go grab her?"

We hesitated. It had been over twenty years since either of us had seen Violet, which meant we were over twenty years older now, and we looked it. Violet, however, looked like she had just stepped through a portal in time and appeared exactly the same—not a wrinkle, not a roll. But even in our college days, standing next to Violet always made me feel like a reject from a leper colony, while Violet always appeared perfect. Every move she made was graceful, easy, effortless. Her clothes never seemed to wrinkle, and she had absolutely no idea what a "bad hair day" felt like. She probably didn't even sweat in the gym. In fact, neither Marie nor I had ever known Violet to *enter* a gym. She was like one of those elegant, taffeta-draped women in a painting by Botticelli. Would a refined lady like that ever be found doing anything resembling a *thrust* or *squat* in a gym? I don't think so. The really wonderful thing was that Violet seemed unaware of herself. Marie and I followed her around like baby ducks eagerly shadowing their mother throughout our junior year of college. Now, observing her in the coffee shop, we were young again, and Violet was our dear friend. Grinning at each other, Marie and I jumped to our feet and hurried across the store to stop her before she could disappear.

"Violet!" we both cried out, as we blocked her path to the door.

"Yes?" Her expression was one of surprise, and she nervously glanced at us, as she attempted to step around us toward the door. "I'm sorry...?"

"Oh, for heaven's sake, Violet! Don't you remember us?" Marie grabbed Violet's arm and we moved in closer. "It's us! Marie and Kay... from school! Remember?"

We grinned at her like a couple mental defectives while she scrutinized our faces more carefully and then, suddenly, she broke into a wide grin.

"Oh my goodness! Kay? Marie?" Violet laughed that wonderful laugh and wrapped her arms around both of us in a big squeeze. "This is so amazing, girls! I never thought I would see either of you again! How many years has it been? Look at the two of you! Still inseparable, I see! Well, well! What a nice surprise! I'm sorry I've been so out of touch—living mostly abroad, you know. Well, for several years I was in Africa! And last year I made some fascinating discoveries in Egypt!"

"Wow! Egypt! Well, yeah, we heard you'd been traveling... a lot," I responded, nodding enthusiastically. "But Violet, look at you! You haven't changed a bit! You look wonderful!"

"Well, I'm only home for a few more days," Violet responded with a little frown. " I'm just getting ready to travel to Pompeii, and then I will be spending some time in Hawaii. The Hawaiian people and culture are so fascinating, and their volcanoes have so much to offer, you know, as a reliable energy resource."

All Marie and I thought that volcanoes had to offer was burning hot, molten lava and instantaneous death. We wanted nothing to do with volcanoes, *especially* the live ones, but not Violet. Violet was a fearless advocate for saving the planet. This was before any of us thought our planet needed saving. She'd been head of every important committee on campus during our college years, and she spent most of her senior year working as an intern for the Elite Energy Efficiency and Cultural Consciousness Global Group... or something like that. Whatever it was, it was real important sounding with a lot of words in the title.

Violet had taken Marie and me in as roommates during our junior year. We happily paid a very modest rent for a wonderful, airy bedroom with two single beds, a big walk-in closet, and a private bath in her charming Victorian house, even though she didn't really need the money. Originally, we had reserved an apartment at a brand new, modern student housing complex for our junior year, but when we arrived to claim it, all our paperwork had mysteriously disappeared. Our apartment had been rented to the daughters of some members of the administration... "*Sorry, girls, there's nothing we can do.*" All our pleadings and arguments fell on deaf ears, and we ended up standing dejectedly outside the building, discussing alternate living plans, beginning with setting up a tent on the lawn of the administration building.

A girl bearing a remarkable resemblance to the genetically gifted "Ginger" from "Gilligan's Island," who happened to be standing on a nearby curb at the time, overheard us. She turned, smiled, and introduced herself. And that is how we met Violet Katz. We all wound up sitting together in a nearby café. Over icy bottles of root beer and plates piled high with French fries, Marie and I bemoaned our homeless situation. By the time we were ready to leave the cafe, Violet had rented us a room in her "modest little house." *Thank you, LORD, for Violet Katz!* Violet grew up in Maryland too, only she was from Chevy Chase—one of the richest boroughs in the country. Her daddy had bought her this great Victorian house near the university, so she wouldn't have to, God forbid, live in the *dorms,* or in a hideous apartment with a bunch of strange people. What her daddy didn't know was that Violet loved all sorts of strange people, and she was ready to have an adventure that included roommates. Violet spent her life as an only child, being carefully groomed, guided, sheltered, and situated in the midst of all the "right" people, in all the "right" places. She was ready to step out into the world and "walk on the wild side."

Despite her strong sense of independence, Violet wasn't crazy about the idea of living alone. She'd been planning to place an ad in the local newspaper requesting *two responsible Penn State coeds to share a house.* We fell into her lap... or maybe she fell into ours, but we were thrilled to have run into dear Violet Katz that day.

How had twenty some odd years come and gone? Marie and I stood there in that coffee shop, just staring at our eternally youthful friend. Violet was so accomplished, and her work took her all over the globe. She had everything. She represented a life of excitement and adventure we'd only dreamed or read about.

And then Violet asked us an intriguing question. "So, where have your travels taken the two of you?" Her eyes cut from Marie to me and back again as she awaited our response.

I could think of nothing. I really didn't think Violet would be impressed with my trip to Bitsy Bexler's wedding in New Jersey.

"Well," I began, "We both married the year after we moved out of your house... well, you were there at our weddings, so you know that! (ha ha... so lame.) And we each had children—I had two girls and a boy, and Marie had two boys and a girl, and we mostly focused on them. Our husbands usually took off together for three or four days in the fall during hunting season. They always looked forward to that. Gosh, let's see. We took the kids to LEGOLAND when they were little and to Disneyland... and we took a vacation to Lake of the Ozarks once. That was kind of fun. But then a year ago we were both widowed when our husbands were killed in an accident. It was during one of their hunting trips..." My voice trailed off.

Violet gasped in alarm and threw her arms around us.

"Oh, my dears, I am so sorry to hear that! Gracious! Are you two all right? I didn't know!" Her voice started rising dramatically. I could see that this was heading right down a detour of depressing details and events, so I quickly stopped her.

"Oh, no Violet—it's all right!" I patted her shoulder reassuringly. "We're okay, really. We've had lots of therapy."

"Yes, that's right. We've had therapy. We're okay," Marie echoed.

This seemed to calm Violet, who appeared on the verge of becoming quite overwrought.

Marie continued. "It was hard in the beginning... but our families have been great, and we've always had each other, so we're okay. We're moving on with our lives."

And then, just like that, I suddenly remembered a family vacation I had taken with my parents when I was ten, and I seized the moment.

"You know, Violet, I *have* done a little traveling! I went to Mitchell, South Dakota for a world famous Indian corn festival once, when I was... well, it was a few years ago, but it was fascinating! You know, the American Indians have many interesting resources... I mean, culturally speaking, they have a lot to offer the... umm... global chain of... environmentally historical... things." I looked up at the ceiling, desperately seeking inspiration. I was so pathetic. I could feel my face flushing, and I glanced nervously over at Marie for help. Marie's eyes were squinting in deep concentration as she racked her brain for some memory of a place of any importance she may have visited. Then her eyes popped open as she remembered one.

"Oh, me as well!" Marie charged ahead. "I traveled with my family to Niagara Falls when I was in high school, and we went over to the Canadian side. The people speak French in Canada of course, so... that's pretty culturally... special... over there, I mean... on the Canadian side."

I rolled my eyes. We wouldn't know *culturally special* if it flew out of the sky, abducted us, and carted us off to Jupiter. We were both pathetic.

Violet smiled gently at us and then spoke as if addressing five-year-olds.

"Well, no, I was thinking more of traveling a little farther out of the country, but certainly the United States has many points of interest... not forgetting the Canadian side of Niagara Falls, of course."

Then we heard a car horn being sounded from the street. Violet quickly glanced at her watch and apologized for having to run. She hugged us both warmly once again and then looked deeply into our eyes before offering her dramatic departing advice.

"Girls, you've *got* to get out and see the world! You can do it! Your children are mostly grown and independent now, yes?"

We both nodded. "Well... mostly," I replied, thinking of Suzi.

My daughter, Susan, had a tendency to call me at one o'clock in the morning from school, angry over some pop quiz one of her teachers had the nerve to administer with no warning whatsoever, or upset over some barnacle-head moron who'd broken her heart. Suzi was notorious for her attraction to needy, emotionally unavailable men whose principal interests consisted of rock climbing, football, and watching "Nick at Nite." Apparently, she was unable to see beyond the beguiling smile and smoldering sexuality *to* the multiple personalities and lack of *gainful employment.* Suzi's last boyfriend complained to her endlessly about the difficulty in finding a decent job. He was finally accepted into the executive training program at Nordstrom's, but he quit three weeks later because there was no way in *hell* he was working on Super Bowl Sunday. Suzi actually felt sorry for him. How could this child have sprung from my loins?

Violet continued speaking eagerly, interrupting my thoughts. "Girls, pick an exotic location and go! Travel to the ends of the earth! See everything!" Violet was practically vibrating, she was so excited. "You'll be fascinated by what you discover! And when you return, I want you to tell me *everything!* Go and have a real adventure!" She reached down in her handbag and pulled out two crisp, cream-colored business cards with her name, title, e-mail, and phone number embossed on the front beneath the words *Global Development of Energy Resources.* We stood watching her, our mouths hanging open as she walked briskly across the sidewalk, turned, blew us a kiss, then climbed into a waiting town car, which whisked her away.

That was it. Violet had become our touchstone. If she could travel everywhere, a single, intrepid, independent woman of the world, then surely the two of us could go *somewhere* new, and maybe even make a difference for good in the world!

After checking out the Red Cross and World Relief Organizations, we decided we weren't quite evolved enough as humanitarians to embark upon a mission to feed the starving children of India or help build huts for the people in Rangoon. For a while we considered an education-based mission, teaching English along with more conservative lip and ear piercing techniques to the Ubangi tribes of Africa. We thought we could also slip in a nice assortment of attractive shirts and blouses for the women of that tribe. Those beaded necklaces they were photographed in just did not provide the kind of coverage necessary to achieve even a tiny modicum of feminine mystique. Most of the Ubangi women also looked as though they could all use a really good bra. We considered these humanitarian based travel options, but they all seemed a little overwhelming, particularly after researching the costs versus danger to human life... i.e. *ours.* We switched to investigating more popular vacation-type destinations around the world and found ourselves drawn to places that were "exotic" and tropical, which meant miles of soft, sandy beaches, endless sparkling clear, blue ocean, and lots of sunshine and gentle breezes. Yes, that sounded much better.

THE SWIMSUIT SHOPPING NIGHTMARE

We decided the first thing we needed for our trip were a few very appealing swimming suits since we would be spending a large portion of time on a sun-drenched beach somewhere, and the swimming suits we owned had been made sometime pre-World War II and sagged to our knees. Since both Marie and I experienced the same mid-life, trauma-induced weight gain crisis, we were on even footing, or better stated, we were each a good thirty pounds overweight.

We began our swimsuit shopping adventure in preparation for our dream vacation to the "islands." Which islands those were, we were uncertain, but traveling to any beautiful "islands" anywhere sounded pretty good to us. Eventually we settled on a weeklong excursion to the Hawaiian island of Kauai. Having solved the problem of where we wanted to go, location was no longer an issue. Locating the perfect swimwear, however, was. We were determined to find perfectly flattering swimsuits that would transform our middle-aged, saggy mid-sections, enormous hips, and bulging bottoms into smooth, firmly shaped youthful ones instead. Surely those clothing design people could have come up with swimwear that could do that by now, we optimistically hoped. We marched through our favorite mall, and into the "Women's Sportswear" section of one of the large department stores, where we discovered racks of sleek, "super-slimming" swimsuits, engineered from the same industrial-strength material NASA uses to launch rockets into space. We selected every style available in totally non-reality-based sizes (they stretch, right?) and headed toward the chamber of horrors, otherwise referred to as dressing rooms. Once we were safely locked inside, Marie and I began the mighty transformation. We quickly discovered that most of the suits we selected were very difficult to get into. I almost strangled myself to death with the first one, a leopard print number, as I tried to navigate a series of shoulder straps which managed to get twanged around my neck. I couldn't figure out exactly how the straps were supposed to go—they crossed over each other in some strange way that looked perfectly normal when the suit was dangling from the hanger. But once the yanking and stretching commenced as I muscled my way into it, I became completely confused as to the placement of the straps. Meanwhile, I heard some kind of barely-suppressed, hysterical giggling coming from the dressing room next to mine as Marie tried on her first swimming suit.

"What's going on in there?" I hissed through the wall separating our rooms.

"I'm not sure," Marie hissed back. "But I don't think this suit was designed for a human. Get in here and take a look at this and tell me what you think!"

I quickly slipped into a swimsuit cover-up I had pulled off the rack for just such an emergency as this and rushed out of my dressing room and into Marie's. There she stood, in front of the mirror in a tiny, one-piece, shocking-pink spandex/lycra costume. The suit had a high neckline in the back, but it dipped dangerously low in the front. Her expression was one that spoke, *Can this be right?*

"Do you think there's a panel or something missing from the top of this suit?" Marie asked. She started pulling apart all the other swimsuits and going through her clothes on the chair, as she searched for an elusive swimsuit *panel* which would somehow *connect* to the front of the suit and cover her generous bosom. There wasn't one.

"I really like the color of this one. It's so shimmery and beautiful. What do you think, Kay?" she asked hopefully as she tugged the suit up.

"I think you have it on backwards," I responded matter-of-factly.

"No, no, I don't think so," she quickly replied. "I looked and checked! The tag is in the back under the neck, and that's always the back, right?" I looked and saw that she was right. The tag was under the neckline in the back.

I studied Marie in the mirror. "Well, what about those?" I pointed to the leg holes. They appeared to be large open ovals, stretching nearly to her waist.

"Well, yes, that is a problem, but look what happens when I pull that part down!" Marie tugged the leg holes down, whereupon her breasts popped out of the suit completely. Now I knew what had prompted all that giggling.

"You see?" Marie looked over at me sardonically. Then, instead of pulling the suit back up, she cupped her hands over her breasts, opened her eyes wide in mock innocence and formed her mouth into a perfect *O*. Her expression said, *Oh my goodness! My top just fell off! How shocking!* In less than three seconds, Marie had transformed herself from a conservative, serious-minded, middle-aged mother of three into... *Playboy centerfold Malibu Marie—the all-American grandmother next door.*

"So, you think I'll get a date in this?" she asked coyly.

"Oh yeah, Marie. I'm sure the officers who arrest you will all want your number." I started to giggle. Marie started to giggle. We both dissolved into uncontrollable laughter. After we composed ourselves, I took charge of the situation.

"Actually, you look a lot like a Las Vegas showgirl, except you need some fishnet stockings and one of those huge, weird feathered head helmets to pull it off. Honestly, Marie, this cannot be the front of the suit. I still think you've got it on backwards. Maybe they sewed the tag in the wrong place by mistake. See how high the neckline in the back is? How about trying it on the other way? Seriously! I think it would look better turned around, don't you?" I hoped I sounded more optimistic than I felt.

Marie pulled the suit off, turned it around, and struggled back into it. Now her breasts were covered, but there was a definite problem with the leg holes around her rear end. The bottom of the suit had completely disappeared between her seat cheeks, and when she turned to face the mirror, we both noticed that the suit gapped strangely down around her crotch area. "Well, *this* isn't right!" Marie grumbled, as she tugged the back of the suit down.

"Oh, whoa, Marie! That's really bad. I'm thinking you had it right the first time. Turn it back around." Marie switched the suit again and resumed tugging the top up. She seemed determined to make this suit *work.*

"Maybe this is a European style swimsuit, Kay. Maybe it's supposed to be real low-cut like this to be more, well... sexy. You know, Europeans are very uninhibited about their bodies. I really do like the color... " Marie continued fumbling with the suit.

"You know what, Marie? This suit reminds me of those wrestling suits high school wrestlers wear... except theirs cover their thighs more. I bet you could get one of those a lot cheaper. You might have to dye it though. I doubt they come in that shade of pink... unless there's a *girl's* wrestling team somewhere you could check into... or, maybe we could add some ruffles... and duct tape," I mused.

"Okay, that is *it!*" Marie snapped. "I'm taking it off! Are you happy now? What about you? Are you having any luck?"

I shook my head. "Not really. I'm going back to my room and see if I can find something that fits." I reached out to grab the door handle.

"Wait just a minute!" Marie interrupted. "What do you have on under that terry cloth cover-up you're wearing?"

"Oh, under this?" I asked innocently.

"Yes! Under that. Come on, Kay! I showed you mine, now let me see." Marie put her hand firmly against the door, cutting off my escape.

"Oh, come on, Marie!" I quickly countered. "It was the first one I tried on, and I was just taking it off! It's really not a very good... look... for me."

"Let me see!" Marie demanded. I slipped out of the cover-up. There I stood in the leopard print suit with the straps all twisted around my neck and right arm, leaving my left breast uncovered. I looked a little like Tarzan in his single shoulder tunic, only in this case, the bottom of his tunic would also have to be wedgied so tight that it would compress *Mr. Excitement* and *the twins* into an area the size of a walnut. The suit might have looked semi-erotic, except that my full-coverage underpants were hanging out of the tiny, undersized bottom, which is never a good look for a girl.

Marie was all business.

"So, what's with the straps on this thing?" she demanded. Marie immediately began tugging the straps apart in an attempt to straighten them. "I think you have your head through the arm hole. Look, this strap is supposed to go the other way..." More yanking and pulling, over my head, around, down, and under my arm... until, finally, "There! That's how it goes," she announced triumphantly as she stepped back. "Well," she hesitated, "it still looks a little strange. What *is* that bulge?"

Marie was studying my chest area. I appeared to have a mysterious object poking out of my sternum. I looked down at myself and assessed the situation.

"Holy Moses, what is happening here?" I murmured to myself. I yanked the top away from my chest and peered down inside the suit. "Oh, good. I'm *not* giving birth to an alien. I see the problem now. This suit has some built-in bra cups, and they are all twisted in here." I freed the trapped cups inside the suit and straightened them. Then I stood before the mirror, pulling the suit bottom down over my rear end. The built-in bra made my breasts look like two rockets in launch mode.

"How come they don't make these bottoms big enough to cover a normal woman's behind, is what I want to know," I grumbled as I tugged the back of the suit down again. It popped back up the moment I let go. "Maybe we could buy some of that tape the Miss America contestants use to keep *their* swimsuits down… what do you think, Marie?"

"Well," Marie watched me with a little frown. "I don't know, Kay. We could try to stretch it a little, or cut off these straps and lengthen them… are you sure you're trying on the right size? It looks a little small. It's only a… oh, it's a sixteen." Marie glanced away as though suddenly fascinated by the texture on the walls.

"This is *not* a size sixteen, Marie! It's a six! It's just that, this must be a *petite* size six. I need the *longer torso* size!"

"Gee, Kay, do they even make *longer torso* swimsuits? I haven't seen any." Marie looked skeptical.

"Oh, forget it. I don't even *like* this suit!" I grabbed my cover-up and hurried back to my own dressing room. I quickly removed the Tarzan outfit and started a discard pile.

The next swimming suit was electric blue, with shiny silver Xs and Os all over it. I thought it might be *the one*, until I discovered I was unable to pull it up over my rear end, which seemed to have grown several inches in the four seconds it took to remove the suit from the hanger. I tugged and yanked and finally decided it would take the Jaws of Life to get this thing on. I peeled the suit back off and searched for a zipper, or ties, or buttons, or maybe a belt, or *something* I must have missed which would keep it from going any further onto my body, but I couldn't find a thing. This suit was obviously designed by some alien from another planet who didn't take into consideration the fact that earth women need garments with openings larger than a light bulb socket in order to get into them. I checked the size. Yes, it was an eight... no... no, wait... upon closer inspection I could see that the suit was in fact, a size zero. The number was smudged and only *looked* like an eight.

"Well, that explains it," I grumbled, as I dropped the suit onto the discard pile. I might not be a perfect size eight anymore, or even a size six, except in my dreams, but no way had I ever been a size zero, except maybe when I was a toddler, or for about three weeks in the eighth grade when I dreamed of becoming a famous supermodel. I thought being anorexic would help me.

My plan was to become so thin and amazing looking that famous model agencies would want me to be photographed in their cutest skinny clothes, which I would then get to keep. I practiced gliding, strutting, posing, and making sexy little turns in my mom's high heels at home until I had my runway walk pretty much perfected. I figured I would quit school and travel the world with my personal entourage and a bunch of cute, yappy little dogs. But instead of that, I just became scrawny and sickly looking.

The boys at school started calling me *zipper,* or worse than that, *Skeletor,* after the scary bad guy on the popular TV cartoon series, "Masters of the Universe," except, in the cartoon, Skeletor only had a skeleton face. He actually had a highly-muscled, powerfully-built body. Skeletor clearly worked out a *lot* in the gym when he wasn't trying to take over the world and expand his evil empire. My face might have been a little thin in those days, but I was no *Skeletor.* Come to think of it, a good plastic surgeon could have helped Skeletor. I don't know. A bunch of collagen and some facial implants might have turned him into a nicer person.

When it came to my supermodel plan, my alleged best friend, Marie, was no help to me at all. She said I didn't have a prayer of becoming a supermodel no matter how skinny I got, because I also had to look either like Grace Kelly, Christie Brinkley, or Jackie Kennedy, and I was just ordinary. Marie told me I better forget the anorexia, model, fame, and fortune program *pronto* and try something more realistic, like becoming an astronaut or the queen of England.

I pulled a peachy-pink bathing suit off the hanger. It had big diamond-shaped cutouts along each side, probably intended to slenderize the waist area. If anything, the cutouts made my waist look *bigger.* It also showcased several of my stretch marks in a most unappealing way. I took it off.

I tried a burnt-orange colored suit that had such a high neckline it qualified as a turtleneck. The bottom not only covered my fanny, but a couple inches of thigh as well. It reminded me of wet-suits surfers wear and looked like it might be made out of polyurethane. I liked that it was so modest and shiny, but it made me look like a big, deformed, plastic wiener dog.

The red and white candy-striped suit I tried next was pretty cute, until I turned around to inspect the back. Either my fanny crack started too high or this swimming suit was cut too low, not to mention the fact that it appeared to be padded on the bottom and was covered with ruffles. It reminded me of looking at the back of a toddler wearing nothing but a loaded diaper, which should have been changed a *while* ago.

The next suit was creamy ivory on top and flared out into a ruby red skirted deal on the bottom, with multicolored confetti-like flecks scattered through it. I thought it would really look great, but instead I looked like a candied apple on a stick with sprinkles. That suit joined the other rejects.

I felt good about the shiny white swimsuit I tried on. It was double-lined, very shimmery, and beautiful… on the hanger. I practically dislocated both my thumbs trying to pull it up, but persistence prevailed. I bravely turned to inspect myself in the mirror. I looked like a fertility goddess for Beluga whales. Word to the wise: never buy an all-white swimming suit unless you are ridiculously thin and exceedingly tan. This was another suit for the discard pile. So far, all I *had* was a discard pile.

Marie started knocking on the wall. "What are you doing in there?" she hissed.

"What do you think I'm doing in here?" I snapped back impatiently.

"Come and tell me what you think about this one!" she demanded. I threw the cover-up on once again and slipped into her dressing room. There Marie stood, in a black bikini, with a bright red bow in the center of the top right between her breasts.

"Have you just completely lost your mind, Marie? Are you trying to get arrested?" I stared at her in disbelief. The top actually fit her perfectly, and it had some sort of push-up bra inside which gave her a very "perky" sort of look. I had to admit the bright red bow was eye catching. The bottom looked like an oversized rubber band wrapped around her hips, while her tummy oozed out like bread dough rising over the top of a large bowl. I stared at her in shock.

"You're kidding with this, right?"

"No, no, no! It's not that bad! Wait a minute!" Marie interrupted. "There is a wrap skirt that goes around my waist like this." She pulled out a black matching skirt with red piping around the edges. She proceeded to wrap it around her waist and tie it over her right hip. Not bad… not bad at all. The skirt covered her tummy rolls and hung neatly around her hips. The black color was slimming, and the suit definitely had possibilities.

"But what about that?" I pointed to her midriff bulge.

"Have you never heard of *crunches?*" Marie sucked her tummy in and smiled appreciatively at her reflection.

"I am going to let this swimming suit be my motivation for getting *thin!* I like it and I'm getting it! Have *you* found anything yet?"

"Well..." I hesitated. "I still have a couple suits to try on. Wanna come in and help me choose?"

Marie stepped into my dressing room. I had three suits left. I tried the next one. It was smooth and stretchy on top, in a beige color, which perfectly matched my skin tone. From the waist down however, the suit material was very bumpy and crinkly. This bubble-bottom was probably intended to disguise or blend in with all the cellulite surrounding it, which is not an altogether bad thing. The fact that it fit snugly around my seat and didn't ride up gave me hope for this au-natural-looking body suit, which just might turn out to be (using one of my daughter's favorite expressions) *smokin' hot.* I wrenched the straps up over my shoulders and turned to inspect myself in the mirror. The first thing I noticed was that my breasts were horribly scrunched inside the tightly stretched top and looked a little misshapen. My nipples, which were visible through the fabric, poked out at very odd angles. My appearance on any public beach in this getup might easily give someone observing me from a distance the impression that not only was I *naked,* but also that I may have somehow managed to insert breast implants into *myself*...while *blindfolded.* The bottom of the suit looked like I had been dipped in glue and rolled in Crunch 'n Munch. I was a large, topless popcorn ball, with horribly malformed gazongas.

"Ummm, maybe this isn't the most flattering... one," Marie gently suggested.

"Geez, Marie, you *think?*" I yanked the suit off as quickly as I could and pulled the next one off the hanger.

Suddenly, a prepubescent sales girl with a figure carved from a potato chip popped her head through the door.

"Hey, Hi, ladies! How are we doing in here?" she asked enthusiastically.

I squealed and threw myself into a perfect imitation of a pretzel, trying to cover my body.

Marie smiled pleasantly at the girl. "*We're* not quite done yet in here," she replied. She stood squarely in front of me, as my personal shield.

"Oh, no problem," sang out Miss Pencil Stick, while smirking at my baggy *big-girl* underpants. "Let me know if I can get you a different *size* or anything!" I hated that girl.

The next suit was bright pink with a ruffly skirt. Once I had it on, I looked just like one of the hippopotamus dancers from Disney's Fantasia. I dumped that suit in the reject pile too and pulled the last one off the hanger. It was a one-piece, halter-style suit, solid black on the bottom and white on top. It had a built-in bra that was intended to lift and separate, which it did. I got the suit on and was a little surprised, pleasantly so, to see that the bottom of the suit hugged my rear end very nicely. (A woman *had* to have designed this suit.) It smoothed my rolls and made my body look longer and leaner. It had that *shape-shifter* quality I'd been looking for. The white top was a nice contrast, and if I had any sort of tan at all, it would look very pretty against my skin.

"I like this one. What do you think, Miss M?" I looked at Marie hopefully. For once she wasn't looking at me like I ought to be swinging from trees or move to Sea World and become part of Clyde and Seamore's Risky Rescue Walrus routine.

"Hmm, well yeah! This looks better, Kay! But what about that?" Marie pointed at my bulging thighs.

"Have you never heard of liposuction?" I frowned at my reflection in the mirror.

"Try squats and thrusts," Marie replied dryly.

"Squats and thrusts... you mean by myself?" I lifted my eyebrows suggestively.

"Oh, yuck!" Marie made a gagging sound. "You are such a total banana! No, I was thinking we need to join a gym or start an exercise program—me for my tummy and you for your hips, Miss Hippy." Marie shook her head at me disgustedly.

"Okay, Miss Spare Tire," I countered, gleefully.

"Although, one should never discuss a diet until after lunch! Don't you agree?" Marie grinned happily. "We've earned it."

We were both bananas.

We completed our diet plan shortly after finishing our hot fudge brownie sundaes. Our diet was going to be a surefire winner. We hurried home to write our plan a little more professionally, via our word processors. The next day was the beginning of *Marie and Kay: Our Amazing Two-Month Thirty-Pound Slim Down!*

THE AMAZING TWO-MONTH THIRTY-POUND SLIM DOWN

"I'm hungry," Marie groaned. "What good is it to plan a great vacation if we die of starvation before we ever get there?"

"Well, this half-grapefruit-for-breakfast plan was your idea," I grumbled. "I don't even like grapefruit unless I can dump sugar on it, and you won't let me do that. Please tell me again, how come we're eating this instead of French toast and pancakes?"

"Because French toast and pancakes will not help us get skinny. That's why," Marie snapped at me.

"You sure are grumpy lately," I glowered at her.

"Well, I'm starving! What do you expect?"

"You know, Marie, we've only been on this diet for two days. How are we going to make it two whole months?" We both glanced at the calendar. There were two big red Xs over April 23 and 24, indicating our successful achievement of the first two days on our diet.

"Okay, Marie, in exactly two months it will be June 24, *magic* day." I flipped two calendar pages over to reveal the month of June. There, the square indicating June 24 was circled in thick, red magic marker. Bold, multi-colored arrows sliced across the page, pointing directly to the circled square. "You see, Marie, this is how much longer we have to stick to our diet. And then, and only then, I get French toast filled with cream cheese, strawberry jam, and powdered sugar, and you get your favorite blueberry pancakes with butter, syrup, and whipped cream for breakfast."

"You're a Nazi." Marie flopped into a chair and stared dejectedly out the window.

"No, I am vain," I replied matter-of-factly. "If you think I'm going to put that skinny black and white swimming suit on this body and walk onto a beach in Hawaii looking like Shamu's *mother,* you can just think again. Now, come on. We have to do our exercises now, and then we get our snack. *That's* the plan."

"Can't we have our snack first? I mean, who will know? Who will care?"

"And you call me a banana," I replied, shaking my head.

"Oh, LORD! A banana would taste so good right now." Marie looked longingly across the room at the large bowl loaded with fruit resting on the kitchen counter.

"After we exercise, Marie."

"Yeah, but if we eat a banana now, we can work it off *as* we exercise!" Marie jumped up and headed across the room to the fruit bowl. "It only makes sense to eat *before* we exercise, so we don't faint along the way. Don't you think?"

"We're not hiking over the Alps, Marie. First we exercise and then we get the banana. It is our *reward* for exercising, remember?" I stood firmly in front of the fruit bowl.

"Kay, are you insane? I want something better than a *banana* for a reward! Bananas are for shipwrecked island refugees who get nothing *but* bananas! They are not for *rewards!* For a reward I want ring dings and chocolate cake! I want donuts and Oreos! I want milk duds!"

"Okay, Marie—you can return to planet earth, now. Here's the deal. Let's *share* a banana now, and after our workout we can each have a fat-free fudgesicle for our reward, deal?"

"Deal!" Marie lunged for the fruit bowl.

We shared our banana and headed out the door for our two-and-a-half-mile walk. It was mid-April, so the weather was lovely, and we enjoyed strolling through familiar tree-lined, well-manicured neighborhoods.

We made it through the first week of our diet, mostly because I followed Marie around with a whip.

Beginning week two, the situation reversed itself. I woke up early Monday morning, *starving.* I threw on baggy shorts and a T-shirt and headed across the street to bang on Marie's door. I could see her through the window sitting on the floor in some sort of meditation pose. She stood and hurried over to open the door. I could see two plates on her coffee table with one grapefruit half on each and two spoons. I blanched at the sight.

"Oh good, Kay, you're here." Marie pulled her front door open and ushered me in. "Do you want to do some yoga with me before we eat our grapefruit?"

"Oh my gosh, Marie! Did you say yogurt? That is a great idea! Where is it? I'm dying fo—"

"No Kay, I didn't say yogurt," Marie interrupted. "I said *yoga.* Do you want to do some *yoga* with me before we eat our grapefruit?

"Oh, nuts. I thought you said yogurt. I gotta tell you, Marie. I need something besides grapefruit when I get up in the morning. Can't we have something else? Did we not have the simple intelligence to offer ourselves any breakfast *choices* on this stupid diet?"

"Yes, we did," Marie reminded me. "We also get a large glass of water with the juice of one fresh-squeezed lemon, remember? We decided that would be the best way to start the day... with a cleansing of our systems."

"Well, the only way I'm drinking a glass of water with a whole lemon squeezed in there is if I can add about half a cup of sugar and a tray of ice... and a couple mint sprigs. They're pretty low in fat, aren't they? I don't know, Marie. Can't we do a revision of our diet and come up with some other choices to start the day?"

"Do you not remember that we already discussed this a million times on the second day of our diet, Kay? We can't eat regular food until after we have cleansed and exercised... fruit only, and *no* processed sugar!"

"Cryminittly! And you call me a Nazi," I grumbled. "Since when do you do yoga, anyway?"

"Bethie sent me this yoga DVD. I just got it yesterday." Marie was just *way* too chipper. "Come on, Kay! Let's try it!" Marie slipped the DVD into the player and soft music started to fill the room. Soon, a beautiful, willowy young woman appeared, standing on a grassy area with waving palm trees and ocean waves lapping gently on the shore in the distance.

"Oh look, Kay. It's *Hawaii!*"

"Oh look, Marie. It's Hollywood with a fake ocean and plastic trees!"

"What is the matter with you today?" Marie demanded. She was quickly losing her chipperness. I immediately felt guilty.

"I'm sorry, Marie. I'm just hungry. It makes me a little grumpy. Let's do some exercises with *Yoga Girl* here."

The gorgeous yoga instructor lifted her arms high over her head and then swept them down as she bent over, stretching all the way to her feet where she bounced lightly, her fingers brushing the ground.

"Holy Christmas! Are we supposed to do that?" I asked Marie. I bent over and stretched, my hands stopping just below my knees. Marie wasn't doing any better. The girl was saying something about treating ourselves gently, with love. I started thinking about gently loving myself with a large bowl of vanilla ice cream smothered in velvety hot fudge and whipped cream with nuts and maraschino cherries, when our instructor suggested we grasp our ankles and gently bounce our heads toward our knees.

"Did I hear her right?" I looked over at Marie, who was struggling to touch her toes. "Did she just tell us to put our heads on our knees? Does this girl belong to a circus?"

"Let's just do the best we can," Marie replied. "In a few weeks, we should be able to do it like her."

"Yeah, try a few years…" I grumbled.

The girl said something about *sun salutation* and brought her hands together at the center of her chest as though praying, which I had already started doing in earnest. Our yoga instructor (I call her *Yoga Girl*) talked about the proper breathing technique. She took deep breaths in and out as she opened her arms wide and then lifted them back up over her head, only to repeat the bend-over-stretching-thing again. After about the fourth time, Marie and I were feeling pretty good about this whole stretching program. I could almost reach my ankles now without bending my knees. We couldn't get the breathing thing quite right because at that point, we were both wheezing, but we continued to try. Then Yoga Girl squatted down and placed both her hands on the ground. She positioned one foot near her hands with her knee up under her chin and her other leg extended behind her as though preparing to take off on a fifty-yard dash. We managed to get in that position ourselves, but then Yoga Girl swiveled her body so she was now facing to the front instead of sideways. She still had one knee bent beneath her chest, and the other leg was now stretched out to the side. She gracefully lifted her hands off the ground and up over her head. Marie and I twisted our feet accordingly, one knee bent, the other stretched out to the side, but the moment we tried to lift our arms up, we both promptly fell over.

"I don't think we're doing it right," Marie commented.

"Maybe we can do it another way," I suggested. We stood up and straddled our legs as far apart as we could and bent one knee in a lunge position that looked a little like what Yoga Girl was doing. We lifted our arms over our heads and waited. Yoga Girl lunged more deeply and placed her left elbow on her "lunged" left knee. She stretched her right arm over her head in a curved arc, which we also did. We doggedly held that position along with Yoga Girl beyond the point of no return, or until we had leg muscle cramp damage so severe, it would require months of physical therapy before we would ever stand or walk normally again. But then Yoga Girl did something that we never would have believed if we hadn't seen it with our own eyes. She removed her elbow from her knee and placed her hand flat on the ground in front of her for support. Then, she slid her bent leg out from underneath her and straightened it alongside the extended one. She resembled a snapped off telephone pole. She told us this was called a "plank."

I thought it was part of a levitation trick performed by the amazing Mr. Wizard. Marie and I just stared at the TV.

"What level yoga class is this?" I asked Marie.

Yoga Girl then twisted her body into a position that looked like she was going to begin doing some push-ups. But instead, she bent at her waist, sticking her fanny up into the air in an upside down V position, which she called a "down dog."

"I've never seen a dog do that," Marie commented.

"Maybe dogs on Mars," I muttered.

Marie and I struggled along, trying all the poses. Then, Yoga Girl knelt down into what she announced was "the child's pose."

"Well, *finally!*" I cried. "Something I can do!" Yoga Girl appeared to be crumpled onto her knees with her head down and her arms resting alongside her knees.

Marie and I immediately collapsed into this pose, and we were just getting comfortable when Yoga Girl stretched out so she was lying flat on her stomach, with her hands at about chest level. She then pushed her upper body off the ground. This she called the "cobra."

"Does your body bend like that?" I asked Marie. "Because, I don't think mine does."

"Just try it, Kay." Marie was actually stretched out on her stomach, pushing her chest up off the floor pretty well. I tried it and heard my back crack in about twelve places.

Mercifully, Yoga Girl crouched back into the child's pose again. We obediently followed her. Then she repeated the snake back-bendy thing again, only this time I just stayed in the child's pose, watching Yoga Girl warily out of the corner of my eye.

Marie and I continued through the rest of the DVD. We decided to keep doing it until we figured all the exercises out. Thank goodness for that child's pose and the standing prayer pose. Those were the only two exercises I could actually do with any degree of proficiency. We had our work cut out for us with this yoga routine.

Marie and I ignored the yoga workout for the next few days in order to give our sore leg muscles some time to heal, and we went on our customary walks instead.

Halfway into our second "diet" week, we both reached the breaking point. It was a Thursday. We were clomping along our normal walking route without speaking, but it was not the easy, companionable silence we usually enjoyed. As often happens with couples or best friends, we spoke at the same time.

"I can't keep doing this," we both howled. We looked over at each other with sad smiles of resignation. We realized we were both giving up on our diet at the same time, instead of alternating quitting, as we had up to this moment. The need to continue halfheartedly nudging each other along was finally over.

"Okay, Marie," I began, "here's the thing. We can't do this diet. We've made it too hard for ourselves. Plus we selected a bunch of foods we hate."

"Yeah, but that was the whole point!" Marie wailed. "We decided on super healthy diet foods we *didn't* like because we knew we wouldn't be in any danger of pigging out on any of it!"

"True," I mused. "But honestly, Marie! Grapefruit? Cabbage? Leeks? Celery? And what was that inedible *crap* you blended a gallon of that first day? What was that... hummus? What is *that?* What good is suffering through a diet trying to eat things we hate just so we won't eat a lot of it, if we become so cranky and miserable we wind up killing each other? Let's just go back to my house and create a new diet. I think we can still keep our calorie count down and portions small if we find foods we really like that are more *filling* or something. Maybe we just need more variety. I've only lost five pounds so far, and I'm hungry all the time. How about you, Marie?"

Marie admitted that she had only lost six pounds. Such a small weight loss after an entire week of suffering hunger and deprivation is very discouraging to any dieter who envisions twenty pounds falling off two days after beginning a serious diet.

We returned home, sat down at the kitchen table, and scrapped our original diet plan, which consisted mostly of water, fresh fruit, cabbage soup... a lot of vegetables we didn't like, and canned tuna tossed in lettuce. We may have actually done well and lost a lot more on that plan if we had just stuck to those food choices, but we sabotaged ourselves the third day by including fat-free snacks. From then on, whenever we found ourselves in a serious food-deprived state, which was nearly every waking hour, we began inhaling boxes of fat-free cookies. Truth to tell, I was surprised we'd lost any weight at all.

"What should we do for breakfast now?" Marie asked. "Can we eat more real food?"

"Well, how about we just mix up the fruits and add more choices? I swear I'm going to bludgeon the next person to death who tries to feed me another grapefruit."

Marie frowned. "Well, my grapefruit diet book did say it was the best fruit for fat burning. What are some other fruits that are supposed to be good for weight loss?"

We both stared at each other for several seconds, and then as if on cue, we both spoke the same word: "*Bookstore!*"

We searched through the cooking and diet section of the bookstore and finally settled on a huge, all-inclusive diet book that listed the calorie count of practically every food known to western civilization. It listed them all alphabetically in food group headings, like Beverages, Breads, Desserts, Fats, Fruits, etc. Then it offered normal serving portions, total fat, and calories. There was also a section on meal planning, goal setting, a chapter on *eating without fear,* and the chapter which ultimately sold us on the book, "*Coping in a World You Did Not Make.*" Perfect. We went home and read the book together. Marie, as usual, filled an empty journal with notes. I just slapped little colored stickies on every page containing helpful information.

Later that evening we had a new diet plan, which looked a lot more reasonable than our last one.

A week went by. The bathroom scale reflected a loss of four pounds for me and six for Marie. The next week those numbers were reversed. We were like bric and brac.

The better we looked and felt, the more motivated we became. Some days we exercised with Yoga Girl *and* walked our two and a half mile trek. We were happy again and ecstatic over our fast-approaching Hawaiian vacation.

I awoke the morning of June 20, feeling tingly and excited. The day dawned sunny and bright. Marie and I were facing our final days before leaving for "the islands." We had achieved our diet goals. I had lost twenty six pounds and Marie had lost thirty. (Marie clearly had a much friendlier scale than I did.) Regardless of scales and measurements, we were both much more slim and toned.

I pulled on my T-shirt, slipped into my new running shorts (although I did not run ever), and walked over to Marie's, where a bowl of fresh fruit waited. We sat on pillows in Marie's family room on either side of her coffee table where our breakfast was laid and began as usual with our morning prayer of gratitude. We sat on our throw pillows after our prayer, just smiling at each other. Neither of us moved. Suddenly Marie jumped up and ran over to her stereo. She pushed a few buttons and a moment later distinct sounds of the islands filled the room with some guy singing something about going back to his little grass shack in Hawaii. I grabbed Marie's hands and we danced around the room. Laughing together, we fell onto her oversized couch as the song finished.

Marie sighed happily. "Can you believe we'll be flying out for our first big adventure in only four days?"

Brim with excitement we jumped to our feet and once again danced around the room. Marie Davies and Kay Taylor were ready to have the adventure of their lives, which was sure to impress our friend, Violet Katz! What a story we'd have to tell her.

DAY ONE: GETTING THERE

Marie and I started to pack the same day we danced and sang to golden oldies on her stereo.

Packing was going to be an interesting experience for me. I enjoyed a very traditional, non-eventful, middle-class upbringing. The Wells's were solid, middle-class, God-fearing folks. There were no skeletons in our closets. Instead, they were stacked with the most disreputable-looking luggage imaginable. When I left home for college, my mother provided me several of these awful *receptacles* for my belongings, which I was too sentimental to throw away. Neil and I purchased beautiful luggage during the course of our marriage, but all those pieces had been taken by our children when they left home. Consequently, on this, the occasion of my first long trip away on my own, the only luggage I could find in our attic was an assortment of containers that ranged from a medium-sized, musty-smelling steamer trunk that had belonged to my father, a sturdy, leather-bound suitcase with sound latches but broken straps, a voluminous puce-colored dress bag which had a hole in the top from which emerged a dangerous-looking hook and a container that looked like a bass drum. This didn't look promising. Fortunately, I had ordered a beautiful set of luggage during my QVC depression days, which was piled in a spare bedroom alongside a mountain of other assorted "must have" articles, also acquired from the TV, right over at Marie's. I hurried across the street to her house.

Unfortunately for me, Marie was as much a stranger to travel as I, and all Jack's and her good luggage had gone to their kids, just as Neil's and mine had gone to ours. I found Marie carefully wrapping her new swimming suit in tissue paper and placing it in the new full-sized suitcase I had purchased from the home shopping network and subsequently given to her.

Marie was humming as I walked into her bedroom.

"Hey, look, Kay! The luggage you brought me! It's going to be perfect! Who knew?" Marie was grinning from ear to ear. Percy Faith's rendition of "The Girl From Ipanema" resonated in the background.

"Hey, Marie, you guys don't happen to have any other luggage lying around do you?" I asked hopefully.

"Well, no... we gave it all to the kids when they left for college, and I never bought more after that." Marie's face turned serious. "Oh, gosh, Kay! Do you not have any luggage?"

I shrugged. "I do have luggage, Marie. It's just, sort of... old, but it's Okay. I can use it." I turned to leave.

"Wait, Kay!" Marie hurried to stop me. "You are the one who bought this luggage—you take it!"

"No, Marie. I bought it for you." I tried to sound confident.

"Oh, that's a big fat lie, Kay, and you know it! You bought this luggage just to *buy* something, and then you brought it over to me, along with a lot of other junk you ordered off the TV because, no offense, you were grieving and mentally unbalanced. Look, there are six pieces of luggage here. I don't need all this. Let's just share it, okay?" I hesitated, considering her offer. It did look like an awful lot of luggage… until I saw the pile of clothes and other travel paraphernalia on Marie's bed. It appeared she was packing everything she owned for this trip. If anything, she would need *more* luggage, not less.

"No, thanks, Marie," I quickly countered. "I think I'd rather use the stuff I've got… for sentimental reasons." I strode out the door and returned to my own house and began packing everything *I* owned in my four sad pieces of… wreckage.

Our day of departure arrived. A half hour before our shuttle was scheduled to appear, I noticed Marie sitting on her luggage out on the curb in front of her house, anxiously watching the street. I maneuvered my non-rolling traveling cases from my front door to the street and joined Marie. Finally, through the pre-dawn mist, we saw the airport shuttle lumbering toward us, and we jumped up and started waving our arms like kids hailing an ice cream truck. The driver of the shuttle pulled up, climbed out, and then stood there staring at all our traveling cases like we had somehow confused him with a driver from the Nationwide Moving Company.

"Are you taking all this?" he asked hesitantly.

"Why, yes!" we replied eagerly.

"We're going on a weeklong adventure to Hawaii!" Marie informed him, with a knowing look.

The man rolled his eyes and shook his head as he hefted my ancient receptacles on board, followed by Marie's sleek, designer black and silver rolling cases.

Once we arrived at the airport, we were quickly approached by an airport porter who offered to lug our bags. We happily agreed and thanked him profusely. When we arrived at the area where we would check our bags and secure our boarding passes, the porter dumped our luggage at the end of a line so long it had to double back on itself a number of times, like a huge conga dance line. Marie handed the porter a five dollar bill. He rolled his eyes and turned to me. I pulled out a ten dollar bill and placed it in his hand with a big smile. He just stood there staring at the bill, and then at me, in a way suggesting that if he had a gun, he would gladly shoot me with it. The porter turned on his heel and walked away. Suddenly, to my horror, I realized I had only handed him a single dollar bill. I called after him while sprinting in the direction he had gone. He turned as I approached and I virtually started throwing money at him, sputtering apologies. I quickly turned away in deep embarrassment and hurried back to Marie.

The line moved at glacial speed. It took us forty-five minutes to get to baggage check in. During that time, I took my humiliation over the porter out on my luggage, kicking it along as we progressed to the front of the line. It cost me an additional fifty dollars to check my bags, due to *excessive* weight, which, in my case, was attributed mostly to the pieces of luggage themselves. Marie had to pay extra for her baggage, too. We decided that this trip might prove more costly than we originally planned. For a few minutes I considered emptying everything out of my traveling "cases" into a couple big, durable drawstring plastic trash bags and throw my strange, mismatched pieces of "luggage" into the nearest dumpster, saving myself the fifty dollars, but time was now of the essence, and we needed to hurry to make our plane.

We managed to get on our plane in time, but then we sat on the runway for about an hour. Apparently a big jet blew out a tire or something and collided with a luggage retrieval vehicle on one of the runways, and we were stuck in line behind about a hundred other airplanes, all redirected to our runway and all ahead of us in the lineup. Finally our pilot announced it was our turn to take off, and we did. Our flight to Los Angeles was long and uneventful. About two hours into the flight, the pilot announced that since we were delayed in getting off the ground, we would be about a half an hour late landing in Los Angeles. Marie and I glanced at each other nervously.

"Gosh, Kay, do you think we'll be able to make our connecting flight?" Marie asked anxiously.

"Well, we better! Geez, you'd think when they know they're going to be late getting someplace, they could just step on the gas. I mean, it's not like there's a whole lot of traffic up here. Can't the plane go any faster?" I looked over at Marie in exasperation. I could see she was also feeling pretty disgusted about our delayed landing situation. We both questioned why airplane pilots couldn't just crank up the speed when they were running behind to make up for lost time. It was a mystery.

Finally the pilot instructed us to fasten our seatbelts as we were approaching our destination. Marie and I craned our necks to look out the window of the aircraft as it descended, staring everywhere in reverence and awe. This was after all, the land of Hollywood and movie stars. The air was so heavy and misty from recent rains however, any spectacular views we might have later reported were mostly in our imaginations.

The Los Angeles airport was huge, and we found ourselves walking for what seemed like hours to get to our connecting flight. As we hurriedly approached what we assumed was our gate, we were told it had been changed and we had to go to another one. We broke into a run as we headed back down the concourse. Suddenly we spotted one of the *ever-present-but-never-available-for-actual-rides* riding carts commandeered by an airport employee who was driving like a bat out of hell and continuously *beep beep beeping* at everyone to get out of the way. Marie bravely stood in the middle of the concourse waving her arms and shrieking for the driver to stop. He nearly wrecked his cart trying to swerve around her and, although reluctantly, he finally stopped.

"Sorry ladies," shouted the employee who was wearing a name tag with *Wendell* printed on it. "I have some seniors on board who are late for a connecting flight."

"Well, so are we!" roared Marie. We hauled ourselves to the back of the cart. The senior couple already seated on the small bench seat was not happy with the intrusion. Marie didn't hesitate a second.

"Sorry, folks. You'll have to scootch over," she announced, as we crowded onto the narrow seat. The senior couple glared at us, but we didn't care. Things were tough all over. Boy, Marie could really get assertive when she needed to.

"We're going to gate C-59 right now, ladies," Wendell shouted over his shoulder.

"Close enough!" Marie hollered back. "We're getting off at C-47."

The driver started barreling along again at breakneck speed, beeping constantly. He barely slowed his vehicle at our gate, so we were forced to catapult ourselves off the cart like a couple desperados leaping five stories from the window ledge of a burning building. Marie flew into a barricade set up to keep people from slipping in a pool of spilled water. I landed on top of her. We both skidded in the water and stumbled into a rack of magazines. The rack collapsed along with us in a heap on the floor. Several alert airport personnel hurried over to help us back on our feet. While thanking them, we dug in our purses for more "gratuity tips," which, thankfully, they refused, and we sprinted to our gate. We barely made our flight. We were bruised and lacerated, but we were safely buckled in when the plane roared down the runway and into the air.

The sun was just beginning to set when we landed at the Hawaiian island of Kauai, touching down on a tiny airstrip that looked like it originated somewhere out in the ocean. We stepped off the plane and drank in the dewy-sweet air that is so prevalent on small, tropical islands. Given the time of day our plane landed, the whole world appeared golden and pink. We sensed the soothing, easy island life, even though neither of us had ever been on one before.

"Whoa... look at this! It's *heaven!*" Marie sighed happily. "Oh, Kay... this is heaven on earth! Could you just die happy right now? True beauty, I knew thee not!" When Marie started rhapsodizing, one never knew where it would go or when it would end.

"Oh, please don't start quoting poetry," I pleaded. Although, I had to admit, the natural beauty of Hawaii was awe inspiring... and this was just the airport.

We headed toward the baggage claim area. Fortunately there were lots of luggage carts available to rent for only a few dollars, so we rented one and hauled our luggage over to the nearest shuttle. We climbed aboard one, which transported us to the car rental place and dropped us off at the entrance.

We stood in line at the *Extremely Cheap Car Rental* counter and waited our turn. There were only two people available to help at the counter and one of them appeared to be "in training." By the time we got our extremely cheap, super tiny, economy, no frills car which practically had to be pedaled, it was dark outside. The lady at the counter gave us a map with directions to our hotel, which appeared to be on the other side of the moon, or about as far away from the airport as we could get.

After arguing for twenty minutes over who was going to drive, we finally flipped a coin. Marie lost—seven out of ten times. She finally accepted her fate, screwed up her face into an expression of unwavering determination, and climbed behind the wheel. Then she turned to face me and waited as I somewhat ceremoniously spread the map out on the dashboard. Since Marie was the driver, I was the navigator. This was not going to be a timely journey, since I was practically famous for getting us lost every time I was in charge of the directions. Marie knew this, but she wasn't any better. After two failed attempts, we finally got onto a road taking us somewhere besides back through the airport. We accidentally happened upon a highway going in what I could only hope was the right direction. The neat thing about driving around an island is that places appearing to be far away on a map are not really far away at all. Soon we were cruising along ever closer to the turn-off, which would take us to our destination.

Our difficulties began in earnest when we departed from the highway onto a "less-traveled" road, which I was positive would lead us directly to our hotel. After carefully steering for several miles along what may have at one time passed for a *road,* we noticed it starting to more closely resemble a cattle trail, which we then tentatively bumped along until it dead-ended. At that moment it started to rain.

Marie stopped the car.

"Oh good, Kay. This must be it! Gee, I wonder where the hotel *greeters* are." She glanced over at me with that *what now* look. I was painstakingly studying the map as though it were a crystal ball, hoping a lighted sequence of arrows would jump out at me, originating from a spot on the map marked with an *X* and the words "you are here."

"I think we need to turn around, Marie." I said, as though our current situation was just a small miscalculation and could be easily adjusted.

"Are you sure?" Marie had folded her arms across her chest and sat there stubbornly refusing to touch the steering wheel.

"Well, I really don't think our hotel is anywhere around here, Marie. I haven't seen any signs or anything."

I glanced over at Marie to see just how mad at me she was. She just sighed as she put the car in reverse and carefully guided it back onto the road. We almost made it back to the road too, but the rain had turned the dirt trail we were on into a muddy bog, and the tires of our car began to spin uselessly as Marie gunned the engine. Finally she gave up, shifted to *park* and we just sat there as the car idled.

"Well, how do you like our romantic tropical island adventure so far, Kay?" Now Marie was really mad.

"Is this just because you had to drive?" I asked.

"No, Kay! This is because you are a horrible navigator!" Marie snapped. "I told you I didn't think that was the right turn way back there when you kept insisting it was. Well, now look at us! What do we do now?" she wailed.

"The lady said to take the second right after the light, Marie. That was the second right."

"Since when did a radio tower signal become a traffic light, Kay? All I saw was that tower signal flashing back there. I didn't see any traffic light. I think we turned way too early, unless we missed the light completely when you said to take the detour after we ran into that construction! Oh, this is great! We're *lost!*"

"Calm down, Marie. I'll get us out of here. I will. We're on an *island,* for cryin' out loud! How lost can we get?"

"Apparently pretty lost with you in charge of the map," Marie muttered. We sat in the car waiting for the rain to let up, but it only rained harder. I decided to take action.

"Look, Marie, I'm going to get out and try rocking the car. Just be ready to gun the engine when I yell *go!*"

I climbed out of the car and immediately fell into a huge pothole. I slogged around to the back of the car and tried to get it rocking by giving it short, regular violent pushes, but it was stuck fast and barely moved at all. Suddenly, I started to fall backwards. In an effort to regain my balance, I reached out desperately for something to grab onto, but there was nothing there. I fell hard on my backside crying out, "*Oh, no!*" Immediately, Marie gunned the engine and thick mud flew out from beneath the tires, splattering me from head to toe.

"*Stop the car!*" I screamed as I struggled to my feet. Marie hung her head out the window to look back at me.

"You said '*Go, go*'!" Marie screamed back at me.

"No, Marie," I hollered back. "I did not say '*go, go*'! I said '*oh no*'!" I stomped back around the car. Rain and mud were dripping off me. Marie pulled a couple big plush towels from her beach bag which, fortunately for me, she had thrown into the back seat of the car along with a couple other smaller carrying cases when we were loading it. She spread one of the towels over the passenger seat and

I crawled in. Then she tossed me the other towel to dry myself with. I pulled off my dripping shirt while Marie unzipped her small traveling case. She handed me a clean pair of pajamas.

"Here," Marie handed me the clothes. "Put these on."

"These are pajamas, Marie."

"Well, this is an overnight case, Kay, so I packed my pajamas in it. It's all the clothes I have in here. The rest of them are in the big suitcases in the trunk. Do you want to go back out there and drag them up here?" Marie asked tartly.

I struggled into the pajamas without another word. I then returned to studying the map as I tried to think of a way out of our dilemma. Then it came to me. "You know Marie, in movies when people get their cars stuck like this they put something under the wheels to get traction... like boards or bricks or something."

"Gee, Kay, that's a good idea. Did you happen to notice any boards or bricks lying around outside the car while you were rocking it?" Marie's sarcasm was really becoming irritating.

"I said, '*or something,*' Marie!"

"Well, since you got us into this mess, you better get out there and find *something* to get us out of here." Marie leaned back in her seat, gripping the steering wheel and staring straight ahead.

"Well... okay then, I will!... just as soon as it stops raining." I looked nervously out the window of the car.

We both sat there as thunder boomed and bolts of lightning crackled across the sky in blazing, broken branches. An hour later it was still raining, and we were feeling decidedly gloomy and more than a little frightened as our car settled into the mud.

"What time is it?" I asked Marie. "I think my watch is waterlogged. It says eleven forty-five. That means it's almost midnight! That can't be right."

"Well, my watch is *not* waterlogged and *it* says eleven forty-five, so it must be eleven forty-five." Marie looked tired and discouraged. "Do you think it's going to stop raining soon?"

"Maybe we should just sleep here in the car and not do anything until it's light outside. At least when it's light, we can see what we're doing. What do you say, Marie?" I asked.

"Do we have any choice?" Marie spoke in a small tight voice.

Marie turned off the car, and we adjusted our seats as far back as they would go. We tried to relax, but it was impossible. Finally exhaustion overcame us, and we fell into an uneasy sleep. I awoke suddenly to a crunching sound outside the car. I shook Marie's shoulder.

"Marie! I think I hear something," I whispered.

Suddenly there was a loud knocking on my window.

"Oh my LORD. We're going to die! Oh, no. *Oh, no!* This is it! It's over! Help!" Marie shrieked as she jerked awake. I leaped up and scrambled into the backseat while Marie frantically locked and then unlocked the doors while pushing the unfamiliar automatic car locks. We both stared in horror at my car door as the knocking on the window stopped and a deep voice cut through the silence.

"Hello in there! Excuse me! Hey, you in the car! I am Officer Kalani, and you are on private property. This is a nature preserve, and you are trespassing! You must move your vehicle! Can you hear me? Do you understand? Please roll down your car window."

I rolled down my window two inches and peered right into a flashlight behind which revealed the face of a wary Hawaiian police officer in a blue uniform with a policeman's cap on his head. He had a gun on his hip, which, fortunately for us, he had not yet removed from the holster.

"Oh! A policeman! Thank heavens you're here," I cried. I had the urge to jump out of the car, throw my arms around his manly shoulders, and sob "Daddy," but I was afraid he might think me more deranged than I already appeared. My explanation of our situation came out in a rush.

"Officer, we just arrived here from America, and we were driving to our hotel, but we took a wrong turn and got stuck out here in this Godforsaken place. Can you help us?" The officer stepped around to the back of the car and suddenly started to laugh.

"This is funny?" Marie whispered nervously.

"I guess he thinks so," I responded. The policeman returned to my window.

"Okay, ladies. I'm going to tow you out of here. Put your car in neutral and just sit tight." The man was still chuckling as he backed a four-wheel drive vehicle to our back bumper and attached a winch. Once we were all hooked up, he eased us out of the mud and onto the road. After replacing his towing equipment in the back of his truck, he suggested we follow him and he would guide us to our hotel. Half an hour and several turns in the opposite direction later, we rolled up to the front of our well-lighted, enormously sumptuous hotel. I tried giving Officer Kalani a hundred dollar bill, but he refused and told us to just be more careful next time and, oh, by the way, Hawaii is still considered to be part of the United States.

We dragged into our hotel and approached the front desk. There was nobody there. We made a lot of noise whistling, clearing our throats, coughing, and saying things like, "I wonder if anyone is here! Hello?" Finally a young man emerged from the back, straightening his tie and rubbing his eyes. Obviously we had awakened him. We told him who we were and that we had a reservation. He stared blankly at his computer screen. Finally he found my name and muttered something about almost giving our room away to another couple since the hotel had been expecting us nine hours ago, but he proceeded to give us the keys and a map to our room. The clerk turned away without another word and disappeared through a door, which he closed firmly behind himself. We looked around for a bellman or a porter or anyone who could help us. No one appeared. Our friendly police officer had left the moment we entered the hotel. We were obliged to remove all our luggage from the car ourselves and drag it like a couple Volga boatmen through the massive lobby to the elevators and down a maze of hallways to our room. It was nearly two o'clock when we finally stepped into our hotel room. We turned on the lights and hurried to the windows which supposedly offered full ocean views. We couldn't see anything as we gazed down except the lighted hotel swimming pool and hot tub and a bunch of tiki lanterns lighting the walkways throughout the grounds, which appeared to be extensive. Gazing beyond the grounds into the distance was like gazing into a black hole.

Ours was a two-room suite, all done in pearly white, pink, and seafoam green. We had a pretty sitting room with a couch and two comfortable-looking swivel chairs, two small end tables with attractive lamps, and a coffee table in the center, on which rested a flower arrangement and a hotel guide. The couch and chairs were situated near two sliding glass doors, which led out to our private deck. The seating arrangement was also near a wall unit containing a big-screen TV and sound system. There was a bar filled with a variety of very overpriced snacks and a number of alcoholic beverages in tiny bottles. There was a mini-fridge filled with cold water, soda, and juice; a microwave oven; coffee-maker; and a safe (like we had anything valuable to put in there.) The other room was the bedroom, and there was a television in there too. The bedroom had two plush queen-sized beds, which were covered in cream duvets with crisp white sheets and down pillows. The closet and double dressers were roomy enough to accommodate our belongings without our having to stack half our clothes on table tops, or live out of suitcases. Off the bedroom was a large vanity area with a huge Jacuzzi tub. It really was the swankiest accommodation we'd ever seen, and we were dazzled.

"Wow," we both breathed out the same moment. "Look at this place." We turned on some soft music, got into our swimsuits and relaxed in our Jacuzzi tub while sipping sparkling cider from champagne flutes. After a while we both started to doze but were suddenly revived as we became aware of the now frigid water swirling around us in our Jacuzzi, so we quickly climbed out and changed into our pajamas. We proceeded to eat two hundred dollars' worth of nuts, chips, cookies, candy bars, and anything else we could find. Then we climbed into our beds, giggling like a couple school girls. We chattered excitedly until sleep finally overcame us and we slipped into happy, hazy dreams of tropical paradise.

DAY TWO: OUR VACATION BEGINS

The next day dawned. I awoke from a dead sleep to Marie gently shaking my shoulder.

"Kay, wake up! You've got to see this! Come on! Hurry!"

I thought for a brief moment that perhaps an alien spaceship had just landed in my front yard to bring Marie so urgently across the street, to my bedside, but then I remembered where we were. I jumped up and hurried after Marie. She had thrown open all the drapes and the sliding glass doors leading to our private deck, upon which she was standing, leaning dramatically against the railing with her arm flung out toward the world beyond.

"Our future awaits! Take a look at this, Kay!"

I did. My jaw dropped as I witnessed a scene almost beyond description. The trees, grasses, and shrubs all appeared to be in bloom. There were a thousand varieties of flowers everywhere, amidst a lush world of green. Palm trees shot straight up toward the sky and swayed gently in the softest, sweetest breeze I'd ever experienced. Past the perfectly manicured grounds of our hotel was a large cream-colored beach and just beyond that, the Pacific ocean, a magnificent world of rolling azure, emerald, sapphire, and indigo. It extended forever and sparkled with what appeared to be billions upon billions of diamonds. We gazed for a long time on this scene of exquisite perfection without saying a word. Finally we turned our rapturous gazes toward each other and embraced, squealing excitedly. This was heaven, and we had been granted entrance.

We returned to our sitting room, called downstairs to room service, and ordered breakfast. We put on our "complimentary" white terry cloth hotel robes, parked ourselves at the little table situated on our deck, and while drinking fresh-squeezed orange juice and nibbling soft, buttery croissants, proceeded to plan our move from Brookhaven, Pennsylvania to this island, upon which we intended to spend the rest of our lives.

Two hours later we were finally ready to leave our room and begin exploring the island. We had received two visits from housekeeping wishing to clean our room and a phone call from the concierge of the hotel offering us a complimentary tour of the grounds and an array of activities we could "sign up" for. We dressed and headed downstairs for our first day of exploration and adventure.

The moment we entered the lobby, we were assailed by two young women with name tags reading *Natalie* and *Nicole.* These perky girls served as activity directors for the hotel, and it was their job to see that the guests of the hotel were aware of and scheduled for all the hotel had to offer. We were sent to join a group assembled on the hotel terrace.

The group on the terrace consisted of a handful of married women with their husbands and several children, a group of seniors bunched together in a large clump, and a pair of younger women who were wearing Michigan State Hockey T-shirts. Then we noticed two men off to the side, talking together. They appeared to be unattached, but one never knew. After standing there a short time, our two female activity guides approached us with exuberant spirits and a formal-looking clipboard and asked if we would care to enter the tournament. They assured us it was going to be exciting and great fun and that Jake Keenan himself was going to be the referee—like we knew who Jake Keenan was. The girls were so excited and persuasive, we found ourselves eagerly signing our names with the enthusiasm of a couple frantic shoppers signing a credit card receipt for the last two genuine Prada bags left on earth, and which were miraculously marked from three thousand dollars down to nine ninety-five.

For all we knew, this tournament could be anything from building elaborate sandcastles to jousting with lances on live horses. But it was the prompting of hotel-community spirit that decided us to sign up. The mention of Mr. Jake Keenan, who had been pointed out to us as one of the most distinguished visitors to the island, further prompted us to make the attempt to participate in whatever the tournament was. Whatever Mr. Keenan was famous for, we saw him as sports nobility. Violet Katz would be impressed when she found out about this. As we eagerly scribbled our signatures, one of our activity guides said this was going to be "sooo fun, simply *tons,*" and we echoed, "yes, tons." Then she said this was one of the hotel's favorite tournaments and we would have a blast. The moment she galloped away we set about finding out what the heck sort of tournament we'd gotten ourselves in for. It proved to be something called *team beach volleyball,* which neither Marie nor I had ever tried before. We discovered that the sport of beach volleyball was usually played by very tall, seriously athletic players, but the owner of our hotel was an avid beach volleyball enthusiast and considered it something of a religious solemnity. Every week began with a beach volleyball tournament for the guests of the hotel.

We looked down on the beach and, sure enough, there was a volleyball net erection ceremony going on.

We finally located a set of instructions and opened them. An insert fluttered out, which I quickly retrieved. It was then we noticed, splashed across the page, a picture of a handsome, smiling, young Jake Keenan. Underneath his picture was a short biography of his sports career. Evidently he had at one time been a beach volleyball superstar.

I think this might be the ideal moment to state that neither Marie nor I are even remotely athletic. We did enjoy co-recreational dance classes in junior high school, but that was primarily to meet boys. When it came to the dreaded PE, we came up with an assortment of rare, tropical diseases to keep from participating in anything more strenuous than keeping score. One year I played girls' softball, only because it was compulsory. My team was the tenth team out of nine, or the *alternate* team, which seldom met, due to the fact that there were no other teams defective enough to play us. The only outstanding feat I ever accomplished in that repulsively degrading activity known familiarly as "gym" was to knock myself senseless once when I fell backwards off the bleachers.

Marie wasn't any better. But Marie was quick and certainly more graceful than I. Moreover, she had bypassed all regulation high school athletics by having talked someone into allowing her to be an instructor in an activity she referred to as "Creative Interpretive Dance." I don't think she had the slightest idea what she was doing, but she had come up with a strange costume that consisted of a tight-fitting vest covered in purple sequins, which she wore over a pink leotard, along with a pair of voluminous hot pink elephant pants. She stuck a rhinestone-studded tiara on her head and adopted several extraordinary body poses to qualify herself as having something *special* to offer. The head of our women's athletic department, a woman in desperate need of electrolysis, named Miss Fleeker, let Marie get away with it. I am not one to write with authority about Marie's class in modern interpretive whatever it was. I attended it only once. Marie, on this occasion, wore her lovely, pink Arabian outfit along with several wispy scarves. The rest of us had to wear regulation athletic attire: baggy T-shirt, one-size-fits-all-shorts with stretchy elastic waistband, saggy white socks, and some tasty footwear known as "gym shoes." Marie had us all prancing, leaping, expressing joy, sorrow, and any other emotion she could think of, while a grim individual named Royce sat at an electric keyboard and accompanied us with such golden hits as "Bali Hai," "To Dream The Impossible Dream," and "I'm Just A Love Machine." Despite my ill-fitting shorts and clumpy gym shoes, I tried my best to act very gazelle-like, but Marie said I was being disruptive and made me leave. To avoid further exertion, I got myself relegated to the defective posture and spinal curvature list, a group of students who were, on their honor, to do corrective exercises at home. Marie, meanwhile, by conducting her class of flapping flamingoes, got out of the suicidal *double-dutch rope-jumping* activity, which was probably a lucky break for all concerned. To my coordinative credit, I had sat on a cow at a state fair once, and I could leap from a spinning merry-go-round without causing any serious injuries, *before* throwing up, and Marie could, with the help of hurricane force winds, get a kite into the air. Heaven knows what made us think we could now play team beach volleyball, unless it was that intoxicating thought of being noticed by a member of beach volleyball royalty.

The tournament was set to begin at eleven o'clock sharp. One of the hotel activity leaders located us standing awkwardly in the odd assembly of people on the terrace and sprinted over. Looking down at her clipboard, she stated breathlessly, "Kay, Marie, you two lucky girls! You're on the first team!"

"First team?" We both croaked.

"Yes! Your match begins the tournament! We're gathering on the beach shortly, so hurry down!" She jogged away, waving her clipboard at a couple other unfortunate participants also scheduled to play.

The color drained from Marie's face. Someone would have to apply paddles to her chest soon if she didn't get hold of herself. To make matters worse, neither of us was dressed for beach volleyball, not that either of us had brought along any beach volleyball clothes. Whatever that sort of clothing was, it had to be something looser and easier to move in than what we presently had on. That particular morning, Marie had dressed in high-heeled cork-wedgie sandals, a red wraparound skirt, and a frilly white blouse which stayed tucked in at the waist only if she kept her arms down. I had on a pair of capris that were a little too snug around my crotch area and a button-down blouse that only stayed buttoned at my chest if I didn't make any sudden movements with my arms. I was also sporting a pair of strappy, high-heeled espadrilles.

I sprang into action, grabbing Marie's arm and yelling, "Come on!" We raced across the terrace in the direction of the hotel entrance and our room in order to dig through our clothes for something looser to wear and more "sports appropriate," but on the stairs we were overtaken by the activity director girls, who appeared to be in a state of apoplectic frenzy. The first match was nearly ready to start, and everyone was waiting for us. I mumbled something about getting into the proper clothes, but they said nonsense, we'd be fine; however, we really must get down there because after all, we couldn't keep everyone waiting now could we? They hustled us back to the terrace where an alarmingly large group was assembling to witness the opening match. We marched down to the sand with sinking hearts. I am one who suffers acute stage fright anytime

I must perform anything in front of people and on this occasion, I had good reason. We noticed four people—two elderly gentlemen from the senior group named Vern and Ezra, who'd probably been dragged away from their oxygen tanks to do this, and the two robust hockey T-shirted girls, Lola and Joan, standing on one side of the net, and two men standing on the other. We were placed on the side with the two men, who were introduced as our teammates, Mr. Jim Rugger and Mr. Stanley Lawrence. We recognized these men as the same two who had been standing together earlier on the terrace. Marie immediately stepped to a position so far away from the net she was actually standing out-of-bounds. She continued carefully, stepping back, and was just turning to make a run for it when the referee called her back. We were all given a short summary of the rules, and Marie and I both nodded stupidly as though we understood. Then somebody pinned small red cloth squares to our backs. The other team had blue squares. As we underwent this procedure, I happened to notice a small, empty dinghy leaning up against a lifeguard tower. I took a position at the side of the "court" nearest the boat—so I could race over, jump in, and row back to California when all hell broke loose, which would happen very shortly. The much-heralded player, who was to act as scorekeeper, Jake Keenan, stood nearby. Marie, in her wedgie high-heeled sandals, wore a fixed grin which might easily have been misconstrued as happy anticipation, but which I knew only too well as a temporary loss of brain function. Her lips curved into a maniacal smile whenever she was terrified. If the pressure wasn't relieved in some way fairly soon, something unusual would happen—in this case I fully expected Marie to throw herself into the ocean and attempt to swim across it. Mr. Rugger eased the tension by motioning to Marie to stand beside him, and she complied. I was positioned in front of Mr. Rugger and next to Mr. Lawrence. Our playing partners were clad in shorts, open-collared sports shirts, white socks, and appropriate athletic shoes. Fortunately for us, our teammates also seemed to understand the sport of beach volleyball as they popped the ball back and forth between themselves for a few minutes before play was to begin. It was clear who would actually be "playing" this match.

It suddenly occurred to me that this must be the hotel organizers' idea of a *suitable* match-up. The two forty-something guys on our team going up against two, healthy young hockey-playing college girls, and Marie and I standing toe-to-toe with two geriatric geezers, who appeared to be in imminent need of hospice services.

Someone tossed the ball to Marie, who in a surprising display of coherency, actually caught it. With admirable control she waved at the crowd, and then she tossed the ball straight up into the air, as though throwing confetti. Her partner, shocked, as if she had just ripped off all her clothes, quickly retrieved it for her. Jake Keenan blew sort of a traffic whistle, and all eight players positioned themselves on the court. Our team drew first serve, and Mr. Rugger relieved Marie of the ball, which he then served admirably over the net. During the first game, our teammates tried gently tapping the ball over to Marie and me, which always resulted in both of us leaping up and down and shouting at each other to "Get it! Get it!" And then we would both swat frantically at the ball and knock it either into the net or completely out-of-bounds. In the interest of winning, our two male teammates started pretending we weren't there, which was fine with us, because we were pretending the very same thing. We spent most of the time just trying to stay out of their way. Even though I only managed to successfully serve the ball over the net a grand total of four out of ten tries, the game was still a walkover for our team.

The hockey-playing girls on the other team were big and strong and they never missed the ball, but they were used to whacking a hockey puck around, which meant they tended to clobber the daylights out of the volleyball, and it seldom landed *inside* the court, ours or anyone else's, and the two seniors playing with them were too timid to do much "attacking" of anything. When they did get a shot at the ball, they tended to hit it in a way that more resembled a bat swinging a baseball, in which case it was usually a swing and a miss.

Jake Keenan called out an impressive, "That's twenty-one for the red team!" and smiled approvingly. The blue team won the second game, but that was because Mr. Rugger and Mr. Lawrence were so tired, they could no longer get to all the balls being flung into our court at all angles by the hockey-playing college girls, even with Marie and I cheering them enthusiastically on. The other team had risen to the occasion and showed dramatic improvement as they played the second game, beating us twenty-one to fourteen.

We huddled up for the third game. Mr. Lawrence was a quiet man with a very steady demeanor and never lost his calm expression, but Mr. Rugger now seemed to lose his generally patient, friendly smile and turned a stern expression upon Marie and me. He told us this game was for all the marbles—or something to that effect. If we lost the third game, we would be the *losers*. If we could win this game, we would win the set and be the champions. He looked gravely at us. "So, are you going to help us win or not?"

I summoned up all my strength and whispered fiercely, "Let's go for the gold!" Marie looked at me as though I had just lost my mind, but when she turned and saw the almost gently appealing look Mr. Rugger was giving her, she whispered intently, "I'll try." That was the best we were going to get from Marie.

We won the first three points handily, but then it was Marie's serve. She had yet to successfully serve one ball over the net. I could see her whispering something in a resolute way to herself. With the most determined expression I had ever seen on her face, Marie tossed the ball up in the air, hauled her arm back, and swung with all her might. The ball flew directly into the back of Mr. Lawrence's head. He was standing no further than five feet away from her at the time. It was the only time during the course of the day that the expression on his face changed. Being a man of great reserve and self-discipline, he didn't say anything. Marie was so horrified at what she'd done, she couldn't speak either. After going over the back of his head with his fingers to make certain there were no permanent dents, Mr.

Lawrence changed places with Mr. Rugger and stepped as far away from Marie as he could. The game continued. Every point after that seemed a dull anticlimax, and, to everyone's astonishment, despite Marie's act of assault and battery, in the end, Mr. Jake Keenan announced that our side had won.

As we all shook hands, Mr. Lawrence looked directly at me for the first time. Suddenly his face flushed a dark shade of magenta, and he hastily turned away. I glanced down at myself and noticed that my blouse had come completely unbuttoned. It was worse than a wet T-shirt contest. My fine, lacy bra, soaked with perspiration, had developed a sort of transparent quality and was now on display for all to see. I quickly began shoving the buttons of my blouse into buttonholes, but they were the wrong ones, which made my blouse gap strangely. Before I could fix it, I noticed Marie. Her wraparound skirt had come somewhat *unwrapped,* and there was a sizable opening on one side, revealing a nice view of her Hanes cotton briefs—the white ones covered with numerous pairs of red kissing lips. She saw my eyes go very wide as I stared at her lower half, which made her follow my gaze down. At once she saw the problem.

"Oh my goodness!" she cried, as she began tugging her skirt over her thigh, but in her anxiety, she pulled too hard. On the second yank, she yanked her entire skirt off. The hotel photographer assigned to cover the tournament had gone into a picture-taking frenzy, first snapping photos of my open blouse and now, one after another of poor Marie's full-coverage underpants. I sprinted over to shield her as she struggled to get her skirt back on, and we half ran, half limped on what was left of our feet from the scene of the crime into the hotel and directly to our room.

Our shoes were full of sand, and our legs and feet were thoroughly coated with it. After brushing all the sand off on our deck, we sat on the edge of our Jacuzzi tub and let cool water run over our legs and feet for several minutes.

Suddenly the phone rang. It was the hotel manager complimenting us on our win and asking us to attend a luau that evening on the grounds of the hotel, in honor of all the winners of the tournament. We felt we had no choice but to agree to attend.

"Hey, Kay! Come check this out!" Marie was standing at our window looking down.

I joined her. Our room offered a very good view of the beach and the notorious volleyball court from which we had so recently escaped. There were eight other poor victims down there batting the ball around. We pitied them and tried to guess which four would be joining us in the "winner's circle" at the luau that evening. It seemed the activity director girls had involved a couple of the families with children in the tournament. It was clear the two teenage boys playing with their mothers were faring better than the two girls playing with their fathers. If these guys were the husbands of the women on the other side of the net, then their wives (who looked a lot like soccer moms) were cleaning their clocks. After a few minutes, we couldn't watch anymore. It was time to find a good pedicurist and get some immediate foot relief.

"THE WUKS"

We limped out of our hotel and hobbled down the street. As we crossed at the corner, we spied the Aloha Nail Salon a couple storefronts away. We made a beeline for the gaudy pink and white awning, anticipating our much-needed foot restoration treatments. Since our fingernails were totally torn and ragged after being bashed repeatedly during the volleyball tournament from *hell,* we decided to get manicures, too.

Back home in Maryland, we'd always gone to a cute little nail shop in downtown Wheaton called Flirty Nails, owned by Marie's aunt Sally. Sally made manicures and pedicures totally fun. She always served us cold sodas and Snickers bars while we soaked our feet as long as we pleased in swirling, warm foot baths. Sally's leg massages were legendary, and she always painted cute little designs on our nails. We figured we'd have a similar, if not identical, experience here at The Aloha Nail Salon. When we entered the door, we expected to see some Hawaiian manicurists working away at various stations through the store, but the only thing we saw were three Asian women sitting together, engaged in animated conversation. Judging from their banter, it was clear that whatever they were speaking, it wasn't English. However their name tags read the very American-type names of Debbie, Becky, and Joy.

Debbie was the first to look up. She smiled and said, "Aloha! I *hep* you?" Marie and I glanced at each other and then back at Debbie, who was waiting expectantly.

"We need pedicures and manicures… and some serious massage treatments," I replied.

"Oh, you want wuks?" Debbie looked at me questioningly.

"What is *wuks?*" Marie whispered out the side of her mouth.

"I think she means, do we want *the works,*" I whispered back.

"So, Debbie, what is wuks?" I asked.

"Today we have beeg special on wuks!" Debbie announced happily. "Vely good fuh you!"

I looked at Marie, who shrugged her shoulders ever so slightly.

"Okay, Debbie! I guess we'll go with that then!" I smiled brightly.

"So you want wuks?" Debbie cocked her head slightly as though unsure of what I had just told her. I began to worry about Debbie's basic comprehension abilities.

I took a step closer to her just in case she was a little hard of hearing and spoke clearly, "Yes! We want wuks!" I nodded reassuringly at her. Debbie got the message.

"You come me."

Debbie motioned for us to follow her, then she barked out something we couldn't understand to her two coworkers, who leaped out of their chairs as if they had just been launched from rockets.

We were seated in two comfortable massage chairs with our feet up on identical foot rests. My massage chair was activated for the roller to move up and down my back in a thumping sort of way, which I quickly readjusted to the "wave" setting which was much nicer. We were also given fashion magazines to read. So far, so good. Then Joy and Becky appeared, each carrying a pot of a gloppy-looking substance that looked like melted caramels for dipping apples at Halloween. I began to wonder if they were going to hand us spoons and instruct us to start eating. A moment later we discovered that it was not delicious melted caramel at all, but melted wax, which had been heated to a temperature of twelve hundred degrees. Becky and Joy slathered this burning stuff directly on our legs. Joy worked on Marie and I got Becky. They used wooden paddles to spread the wax over a small area of our legs, then they placed a strip of material over the wax, and suddenly, they ripped the strip off, along with a couple layers of our skin. Marie's face turned ashen, and I yelped in pain. Before Becky could dump any more of the molten wax on me, I jerked my legs away.

Becky looked confused. "*Is too hot?*" she asked.

"Yes! Is too hot!" Marie and I cried in unison.

Becky and Joy grabbed their bowls, ran to the back of the shop, and disappeared into another room. We could hear them jabbering in their native language—whatever that was—along with excessive giggling. When they emerged from the back room moments later, they looked quite serious as they approached us.

Becky said, "Now wax coolah, okay?"

"Yes, Becky," I responded. "*Coolah* is *bettah.* Thank you."

The wax was maybe two degrees cooler the second time it was spread on our legs. Marie looked miserable as she turned to me.

"Hey, Kay, they really should give you some Demerol or Morphine, or at least a general anesthetic before they do this," she whimpered.

"I think we're going to need some kind of post-traumatic stress therapy like those guys who get shot at in the war before we get out of here," I grumbled.

"What war?" Marie whispered.

"Any war," I responded, grimacing, as Becky ripped off another section of my leg.

The only good thing about our leg waxing experience was that Becky and Joy were efficient and fast. When they finished, our legs were red and blotchy but smooth as silk.

Then Becky started pointing at my crotch, saying something that sounded like, "Biki wax fuh you?"

I looked over at Marie who looked like she was ready to bolt for the door. I turned my gaze back upon Becky.

"You know, Becky, I don't know what a *biki wax* is, but I'm pretty sure we don't want it."

Becky dashed across the room and returned with a poster which quite adequately pictured what the "biki wax" was. The poster was of a beautiful young woman wearing a very skimpy bikini. The phrase "*Get a bikini wax today and look hot in your sexiest swimwear,*" was splashed across the page, and several arrows pointed directly at the model's very smooth, barely concealed hoo-ha area. The girl on the poster was laughing and holding, of all things, a volleyball.

Marie began shaking her head emphatically as she spoke, "No biki wax! *No biki wax!*"

Becky and Joy seemed to comprehend that we were *not* wanting the "biki wax." Joy took the pots away and disappeared. We were then led to two new massage chairs. At the base of each was a deep-foot bath filled with swirling water. This was what we had been waiting for. Unfortunately for Marie and I, the water into which we attempted to insert our feet was hot enough to melt stainless steel.

"Yipes!" I yelped, as I jerked my feet out of the bath. Marie also had her feet pulled up and was gently fanning them, sending little messages of comfort, healing, and love.

"Watah too hot?" Joy asked.

"Yes, Joy, watah too hot!" Marie sternly responded. Joy quickly turned a valve on both our foot baths and cool water poured in. Moments later our feet rested in more comfortable baths. Our massage chairs were relaxing our stiff, tired backs, and the water swirling around our feet and ankles was soothing and pleasant. The girls brought over several trays of nail polish and we selected a very neutral polish called Barely There for our toenails.

Suddenly Becky grabbed one of my feet and hauled it out of the warm water onto a foot rest. I looked over at Marie who was experiencing the same unwanted interruption to her far-too-brief foot soak. Becky and Joy patted our exposed, frigid feet dry and began digging and poking at our toes. Evidently Marie had some ingrown toenail issues, because she nearly exploded through the back of her chair when Joy began digging on the side of her big toe.

"Holy mother of mercury, Stop that!" Marie hollered.

Joy looked up at her with drawn eyebrows.

"Oh, solly," was all she said with a little shrug.

"Well, you're going to be a lot more than sorry if you do that again," Marie warned.

"Gee, Marie, they don't do it like your aunt Sally, do they?" I whispered.

"Do ya think?" she snapped. I could tell Marie had run out of all her good behavior.

Once the digging of the toes and toenails ended, Becky and Joy began rubbing and scrubbing the soles of our already tender feet with a couple of small, hard, coarse Machiavellian torture sticks.

"Ouch! What's that?" I demanded.

Becky calmly looked up at my crazed expression. "This fuh callus."

I looked over at Marie.

"Hey, Marie, don't you think two hours of jumping around in gritty sand already took care of our calluses?"

"You'd think so," Marie agreed. "Ouch! Geez, Joy, I don't have calluses on my *ankles.* Cut it out!"

Marie was no longer even pretending to be nice.

She turned to me and said, "You know, for somebody named *Joy,* this girl sure isn't bringin' any in here." Apparently Marie had stopped caring whether these nail salon workers could either hear or understand her.

I jerked my foot away from Becky as she started scraping inside the sensitive, non-callused arch of my foot, and with emphatic gestures, both Marie and I cried, "No more callus. Please stop!" At this point we were afraid to lower our feet back into the hands of our pedicurists. They must have taken pity on us because they put their callus-removal implements of torture away.

They proceeded to pull out what looked like bottles of lotion. Marie and I both held our breath hoping we might now get our legs and feet massaged. What a relief! Our pedicurists squeezed long stripes of lotion on our legs and began stroking and massaging them. Heaven. Once again we relaxed back into our chairs to enjoy the experience.

Twenty seconds later, my relaxation came to an abrupt halt when Becky began whacking my legs with aggressive karate-chops.

"Why are you doing *that?*" I cried out as I winced in pain.

"Massage nice, huh?" Becky smiled benignly. I had no idea where Becky actually came from, but on planet earth, we did not find *leg whacking* to be particularly "nice."

"No, not nice! Stop that!" I held my hand out, hoping she understood basic sign language for the word *stop.* She went back to massaging my legs. I glanced over at Marie. Her eyes were closed and her face was turning red from the exertion of holding her breath as Joy manhandled her legs.

"Marie," I hissed. "What are you doing?"

"Shh! I'm concentrating. Do you think she'll stop soon?" Marie asked tightly. As if by magic, Joy stopped maniacally squeezing and kneading Marie's screaming calf muscles. She dipped her hand into a bucket of some grainy mixture and started rubbing it firmly onto Marie's feet.

"Oh, dear God, please help me," Marie croaked.

"What are you doing now, Joy?" I anxiously inquired.

"Oh, this? This salt rub—fuh feet!" Joy announced happily.

When I noticed Becky loading her hands with the same salt mixture and preparing to rub it on my feet, I held my hands in a "time out" position and said, "Okay, girls, *no more!* All finished! Massage over now. All done... thank you."

They immediately stopped, reached over, rinsed and dried our legs and feet, and grabbed the bottles of nail polish, which they then applied to our toe nails. Finally the leg and foot part of our "wuks" experience was over. We were next led to chairs at small tables for our manicures.

"Do we really have to do this?" Marie looked at me pleadingly.

"Look at your hands, Marie."

In order to save on expense, we had purchased and applied a couple sets of inexpensive press-on nails prior to our vacation and, needless to say, only a few of the nails were still pressed on.

"Okay, maybe you have a point," Marie responded in sad resignation.

Becky sat down in front of me, and Joy reached for Marie's hand.

"Ouch!" Marie cried. We all froze. Joy looked quizzically at Marie, who suddenly realized Joy hadn't done anything except take her hand. "Oh, sorry, Joy. I was just a little nervous," Marie spoke apologetically. "You may proceed. Just be… gentle, okay?"

"Manicue vely nice, you like?" Joy asked.

"I think I'd like it more if you spoke and understood a little more English…" Marie mumbled. Joy's smiling expression didn't change.

Becky and Joy began removing the rest of our press-on nails, clucking and chattering with each other in their own sort of singsong, nasal sounding language as they did. A few more giggles escaped during their exchange. Then they prodded and poked at our fingernails with little nippers, files, metal shapers, and buffers. We turned down the acrylic nail experience. Outside of childbirth and a couple emergency trips to our dentist, Doctor Drillmaster, and his agony-inflicting instruments of death, we had never been subjected to torture in our lives and lacked the necessary courage to suffer anymore at the hands of Joy and Becky, employees of the Aloha Nail Salon.

Becky applied a soft pink polish to my nails, and Marie opted for bold red. It would go nicely with the red bow tacked right between the breasts of her swimming suit top.

One hundred and twenty-five dollars apiece later, we finally stumbled back out onto the street. We were exhausted and shaken from the ordeal, but all our nails were nicely shaped and polished.

THE LUAU

After arriving back at our hotel, we discovered a full-service spa on the second floor. We spent the rest of the afternoon there where we received heavenly massages, complete facials, and new hairstyles. We then ventured out into the shops near the hotel, where we discovered an amazing array of souvenirs to buy, but what we were really looking for was Hawaiian "luau attire." One sales girl directed us to a clothing shop nearby, and her instructions were so good that we actually found the place without getting lost.

Inside the clothing shop, we found racks of traditional muumuus in quite a few styles and some beautiful sarongs mixed in. We finally settled on a couple long, silk sarong dresses and beautiful coordinating wraps. The sarong dresses were more formfitting and slenderizing than the muumuus. They tied at the waist, which accentuated our waistlines. The shoes we had worn for our beach volleyball event were ruined, so we bought new sandals, too. We were now ready to be honored at the evening's beach volleyball championship ceremony. As we admired ourselves in the mirror of the store, dressed in our new finery, I envisioned

Marie and I rising, smiling, and nodding to all our "fans" at the luau. Maybe, with our new dresses, shoes, hairdos, and freshly-polished nails, we'd catch the eye of a couple handsome, available, retired jillionaires who'd be so smitten they could do nothing but beg us to join them in holy matrimony for the rest of our lives.

We arrived back at our hotel suite with just enough time to change clothes for the luau. Then we dragged a member of the housekeeping staff into our room to take several pictures of us dressed up and standing together on our deck with the sun setting in the distance. Marie leaned on the rail, gazing romantically at the ocean and quoted the only sea poem she had ever learned at school, "The Wreck of the Hesperus," by Longfellow. She quoted the whole thing, which I considered (and still do) extremely elaborate of her, not to mention completely bizarre considering our surroundings. The poem contained phrases like, "The snow fell hissing in the brine, and the billows frothed like yeast," and expressions like, "stinging blast, cruel rocks, and bleak sea beach." Maybe the ocean surrounding this lovely Hawaiian island could get a little rough at times, but I highly doubted that snow fell hissing anywhere around here, and the beach was anything but "bleak."

When Marie had completed her emotional orgy, we headed downstairs for the party.

As we entered the lobby, Natalie, one of the activity directors, spied us and charged across the room to where we were standing.

"Kay, Marie, you're here! Great! We have a wonderful evening planned for you! I'll be your guide. Let me show you where you'll be sitting!" She linked arms with Marie and I and marshaled us out past the patio, onto the grounds where a number of tables were set up. Ours was right in front of the stage. She then guided us away from the tables to an area where a large number of people were gathered. Something significant appeared to be happening.

"Here we are at the centerpiece of the luau!" Natalie chirped happily. "We are just in time to watch the unveiling of the Kalua pig!" She continued to explain the procedure. "The pig is stuffed with fiery hot lava rocks, and then wrapped in moistened burlap bags and *ti* leaves. It is surrounded by more hot rocks and roasted all day in the pit you see here. It's quite an involved preparation, practiced for generations by the Hawaiian people!"

Marie and I watched as several young Hawaiian men dressed in ceremonial costumes removed the pig from the ground. After a few minutes, Marie whispered something about going to get something to drink, and that was the last I saw of her for the next half hour.

After the pig was gathered up and removed, the onlookers began moving off. I started searching for Marie. I located her over by the bar, engaged in animated conversation with quite an attractive, older man. From the way he spoke, he must have been Australian, in fact, so much so that when he spoke, I could barely understand him. Marie, not to be outdone, had launched forth into a novel accent of her own. Suddenly she sounded amazingly like Scarlett O'Hara straight out of *Gone with the Wind.*

As I approached, she turned to introduce her stunning new conquest. It was clear she had no idea of his name, but he was ruggedly handsome, and the glitter of gold braid and brass buttons on his uniform and service cap made her feel she should at least mention his rank. I'm sure she imagined him to be the captain of some luxury ocean liner or at the very least, an airline pilot on leave.

"This is mah best friend, Missuz Kay Taylah, Cap… er… Offi… er, Command… er… Admir… "

The man put an end to her floundering by introducing himself. He barked something in my direction that sounded something like "Shitts Yoda." My smile froze. Maybe he said *Ships Odor?*" No, that couldn't be right. Maybe it was *Chitts* something? I finally guessed his name to be Chips O'Dell… or O'Toole? Either of those made more sense, because the alternative was not anything a rational thinking mother would name her child. In any event, *whoever* he was, he coolly appraised me from head to toe, then quickly turned his attentions back to Marie.

She was asking him what he thought it was like to be captain of the *Titanic,* like maybe he had served on board *that* ship. Then she switched to the subject of air travel and how terribly courageous the pilots manning those huge commercial jet planes must be. In the meantime, he was attempting to steer the conversation to where she lived, or better yet, the location of her hotel room. Marie, who somehow didn't think that he'd know about Brookhaven or even Pennsylvania, had given as her general address the entire continent of North America. After a few minutes, the gentleman produced from his jacket a few photos of whom I presumed were his family. This I felt had the earmarks of a very sticky situation for Marie. I whispered that

I was going to find a ladies' room and ducked away. I wondered, as I went, if Marie had introduced herself as *Mrs.* Marie Davies, or merely as "Marie."

Our trip of independence had truly begun. There were no husbands, no children or parents to cramp our style, whatever that was. Before us was something I liked to think of as our new beginning. Who knew what delectable adventures awaited us? Even now, Marie was embarking on what might blossom into... who knew? Knowing Marie, I doubted anything suspicious would happen with Captain Chitts. I recalled the snapshots of whoever back in wherever and thought how conscience-stricken Marie would be if that were his wife and kids. She'd never pull it off. Maybe the pictures were of his sister and the children were his nieces and nephews. I doubted it. Not in a million years would Marie be that lucky. I started to wonder if there might be some unattached, amazingly handsome man I could enchant by doing something typically *me,* like accidentally tripping him into a shark tank or into the back of some guy walking on stilts.

My husband and I had speculated from time to time during our marriage about what would happen if either one of us died. We hadn't been very serious at the time, but maybe we should have been. I always told Neil if I died before he did, I would never want him to be alone and that I hoped he would get married again... to Golda Meir, Mother Teresa, or Wilma Flintstone. Neil also suggested highly non-available or non-living men for me, like Walter Cronkite, Dick Clark or the Pope. Regarding this Hawaiian adventure however, it was clear my best friend had obviously bagged the most distinguished looking man around. I tried to picture Marie in an old-fashioned "make out" session with Captain Chitts. My reverie was cut short, however, when I noticed Marie hurrying in my direction, looking quite put out with me. The only time Marie and I ever became unpleasant with each other was when we found ourselves in awkward situations—usually of our own making.

I spoke tentatively, "What have you done with your admiral or commander, or whatever?"

"I haven't done anything with him," she snapped. And, he isn't an admiral or any of those other things.

"Oh." There was a pause.

"He isn't anything."

There was another pause and then the truth came out.

"Not only is he *married,* but he's a *chauffeur.* It's his chauffeur's uniform. He's the driver for Mr. Keenan. They're both from Australia. He asked me if I'd like to get better acquainted with him in the back of his limo."

My only reply to this was another "Oh," and to avoid further embarrassment, we both turned and looked away.

We wandered over where people were starting to fill their plates at the dinner buffet. There were enormous platters of food spreading into the distance over several long tables. There was no way any one person could manage even a tablespoon of each dish and have room enough on one plate to sample everything. It was an outrageous amount of food. It also looked quite delicious. We carefully organized our portions to utilize the largest number of dishes to fit on our plates. Someone told us we *must* try the poi. It looked a little like mashed oatmeal or puréed parsnips. We tentatively put a spoonful on our plates. Who knew? Maybe it was ambrosia of the gods and the most delicious taste experience of our lives. We might wish we had loaded up on the stuff. I added a little extra to my plate, just in case. We balanced our coconut cake-filled dessert plates atop our overladen dinner plates and carried them in one hand while carrying our drinks in the other.

Our table held ten people. Marie and I were seated together, with Mr. Rugger strategically placed on Marie's left and Mr. Lawrence on my right. The other four winners, two teenage boys with name tags reading C.J. and Spike, sat across from us with their soccer moms, Roberta and Amy. The owner of the hotel sat with the illustrious Mr. Jake Keenan between the two groups of winners. At first, all ten of us said nothing, and I began to feel I was back at school in science lab sitting before a dead frog. Eventually I looked over and noticed the legendary Jake Keenan, dressed in a Hawaiian shirt with hula dancers all over it, looking my way. It must have been some years since he acquired legendary volleyball playing status, because he was now around fifty, a little paunchy, and had hair plugs. He said something about what a fine tournament it was, and didn't we all play well. I immediately looked behind me to see who he was speaking to, because it couldn't possibly be me. Mr. Rugger cleared his throat, and Marie glanced over to see him gazing intently at her. He asked if he might trouble her for the salt, and she burbled how it was no trouble at all and how *happy* she was to get it for him. He smiled and blushed a little, and then she blushed.

I wondered what the heck was happening here. Since when did a simple request for a condiment turn into hot and heavy sexual chemistry, and how come I wasn't getting any? When Marie passed him the salt, I noticed his hand brush hers as he accepted it. She reacted as though he'd just French-kissed her. Her face turned bright red, and she kept glancing down at her plate in great consternation. I thought maybe a giant bird had pooped on her cake or something. Suddenly Marie launched into a moving discourse, telling Mr. Rugger how brilliantly she thought he had played the volleyball match that morning, how well he moved, and that he must be a professional volleyball player or something. I couldn't believe Marie was actually saying this crap. Anyone watching our game that morning could easily see that our male teammates were non-volleyball players, beach or otherwise, and were just giving it the old "college try," if they could remember back that far. Mr. Rugger returned the compliment by saying that Marie had really come alive there at the end and made some critical points herself! That was it. I was now convinced that aliens had taken possession of both their bodies. I was also pretty sure that crop circles were real and Elvis was alive and well... and probably among the guests at this party.

Marie was now disagreeing rather strenuously that, no, whatever she had done was because Mr. Rugger had been there helping her, making her look good, and he said no, not at all. I looked anxiously around the room. Nobody was levitating or anything. No one else appeared as though anything unusual was going on at all. In fact everyone else at our table had started talking to each other, so I turned my attention to the man sitting on my other side, Mr. Stanley Lawrence. He didn't say anything, and I came to the conclusion that either he was the strong, silent type, or maybe he was just suffering from brain damage after having a volleyball launched into the back of his head. Just as I began to turn away, he spoke, "So, you're Marie, is that right?" *Geez. Could this guy not read a simple name tag? LORD, this was going to be a long night.*

"And you are Mr. Lawrence," I responded politely.

"Please, call me Stan." He smiled and held out his hand, which I took. He had a warm smile that crinkled his Paul Newman-esque blue eyes in the most appealing way. I wondered why he didn't smile more often.

"Well Stan, in that case, you can call me Kay," I replied.

He hesitated. Then, suddenly realizing his blunder, he said, "Oh, no, I'm sorry! It's just that you don't have a name tag, and you really look quite *different* now than you did this morning." I quickly glanced down. Sure enough, my name tag was gone. Somewhere along that football field of a food train, probably floating in a huge vat of *poi* was my nametag.

"No, I think I should be the one apologizing." I mumbled, embarrassed.

"Not at all. We did play the tournament together, if you could call it that. I should have remembered your name. So, *Kay,* here we are, sitting together at a luau in Hawaii. We could begin by telling a little about ourselves. Would you like to go first?"

"Well, *Stan,* my whole name is Kay Elizabeth Taylor, no relation to Hollywood royalty, by the way. I'm vacationing here with my best friend, Marie Davies, who is sitting next to your friend—you remember Marie—the one who served the ball into your head?"

He laughed. "Oh yes, I remember her—quite lethal with a volleyball."

"Anyway," I continued, "Marie and I live in Pennsylvania, but we're from Maryland originally. We grew up together and met our husbands at college. They were roommates and good friends, just like us. We married around the same time, settled in the same area, had our children, who are now grown up, but we were widowed a little over a year ago when our husbands were killed in a highway accident. And..." I shrugged. "That's about the whole story."

He looked away and paused a moment before replying. "I think there is a lot more to that story."

"Well, yeah, but it's boring," I countered.

"Doubt that." Stan returned his gaze to me, a slightly wistful smile playing on his lips—ooh, I could get used to those. He continued, "I'm sorry about your husband. I lost my wife Janice to cancer three years ago, so I know something about losing a spouse. My buddy Jim over there is divorced, and he and I own a sports supply company in Phoenix, Arizona, where we also live. And, that's about the whole story."

We both laughed then, and that stretch of ice was broken. We continued chatting as we plowed through the mountain of food on our plates. Eventually I arrived at the little mound of Hawaiian *poi.* I scooped up a large forkful and popped it in my mouth. My thoughts about "ambrosia of the gods" were immediately replaced with thoughts of Marie's *special* low-fat Anchovy/Velveeta Vegetable Dip and melted pencils.

Stan raised his eyebrows. "So, what do you think?" He had the nerve to chuckle as he observed my expression. "It tastes like wallpaper paste, right?"

"What is this?" I choked as I grabbed my water glass and quickly drained it.

"It's *poi.* It's made from fermented taro root—it's sort of bitter and... different. It's an acquired taste. It's just that not many of us from the mainland care to *acquire* it."

We were halfway through our desserts when a man walked to a microphone in the center of the stage. He announced that it was time for our evening's entertainment and introduced a local group of Hawaiian dancers. He then exited the stage, and a dramatic beating of drums filled the air as beautifully costumed Hawaiian girls filed on stage. They performed a number of dances, which made them all appear to have some kind of special hip-dislocation abilities. After the girls finished, several male dancers came on stage and performed. Then, the all the dancers performed together. The last number was one young man performing with fire batons, which created a strong climactic finish to the show. The music stopped, the drums and applause ceased, and the stage fell silent. We noticed several of the dancers quietly filing back on stage and just standing in the background as the owner of the hotel, Mr. Robert Sinclair, jumped up from his seat and hurried on to the stage and grabbed the microphone.

"Good Evening!"

His deep voice resonated through the crowd.

"We have a special treat for all of you tonight," he continued. "We have several *very* special guests we'd like all of you to meet," he continued, his voice rising as he spoke. "This morning we witnessed another historic beach volleyball tournament right here at the beautiful Hotel Kauai, and the winners of that tournament are all with us here tonight!" He gestured grandly toward our table and continued. "We all enjoyed watching them win their matches on the beach volleyball court this morning, and we are going to have the rare privilege of watching them perform for us again! Would you like to see that? Come on up here, you volleyball superstars!" The crowd went wild.

I looked at Marie. She looked like a deer caught in headlights. Her face was frozen in that crazy smile again. Even though we all knew *something* would be said about the tournament, none of us thought we would have to *do* anything more than sit at our table, smiling, while everybody politely clapped for us. I considered climbing under my chair and just crawling away, but bright spotlights were swooping through space and locking directly upon all of us at our table. Mr. Sinclair continued urging us up on stage. By now everybody in the place was clapping and cheering. Reluctantly we stood and made our way on stage. The announcer drew everyone's immediate attention to the illustrious Mr. Jake Keenan and proceeded to make quite a fuss over him. Jake smiled happily and waved at the crowd and then at the photographer taking pictures. The rest of us were introduced, and pictures of us were flashed on a huge screen. There was one of Marie reaching back to serve the ball. Fortunately it did not go on to show what happened to the ball after she hit it. There was one of me jumping up and reaching for an incoming ball. It did not show me missing it entirely and falling flat on my face. In the background of the shot was Mr. Lawrence in mid-stride coming up right behind me. It did not show him actually hitting the ball after I missed it. Mr. Rugger's picture was of him serving the ball perfectly from the baseline. The other winning team had similar performance shots for all to see. When the introductions and pictures were over, it was time to honor us with a special Hawaiian dance. That was all well and good. I started heading toward the stairs at the side of the stage, relieved that my moment of awkward embarrassment was over, but this was not to be. The announcer told everyone that this next dance was *particularly* special because all the winners on stage would be participating. More ecstatic clapping, wolf whistles, and cheering from the crowd followed. Evidently, we were trapped up there. The music came alive, the drums started pounding, and the Hawaiian performers started dancing as one toward us. I started to wonder what happened to the tournament *losers.* Maybe they were just taken out and shot. The lovely Hawaiian girls danced over to Marie and I and the two soccer moms standing there, while the male dancers danced over to Mr. Keenan, Mr. Lawrence, Mr. Rugger, CJ., and Spike. We all had Hawaiian leis placed around our necks, and our Hawaiian dancing "instructors" started indicating for us to follow their movements, which we all did. I immediately felt sorry for Mr. Lawrence and Mr. Rugger, who were shown a strange-looking chicken dance in which both knees were bent, moving apart and together along with some hip thrusting thing, which looked comical at best. This was the Hawaiian fertility dance, and our guys were awful at it. We women were shown the traditional female Hawaiian hip swing and arm waving hula dance. I think the arm movements were supposed to resemble the gentle waves of the sea, but mine looked more like I was trying to flip something disagreeable off the backs of my hands. I looked over at Marie who had her hips swaying practically like a native. I suddenly wished I had tried a little harder in her modern interpretive dance group. I was just starting to get my hips going when I noticed the female Hawaiian dancers gradually moving us toward our male teammates. The male Hawaiians demonstrating for these guys suddenly disappeared, and I found myself directly in front of Mr. Lawrence, and Marie was standing with Mr. Rugger. The only one of us still anywhere near a professional dancer was Mr. Keenan, who was having the time of his life dancing with a beautiful, young Hawaiian girl with coconut shells placed strategically over her breasts. The way he was dancing, I started wondering if he might be legendary at more than just volleyball. Marie suddenly abandoned her hula dancing and just stood there watching in stunned silence as Mr. Rugger repeatedly thrust his hips at her in what some might consider a *suggestive* way. Suddenly he looked up and saw her. So focused had he been trying to get his Hawaiian fertility dance perfected, he didn't realize his Hawaiian male dance teacher was no longer there, and he was now standing on a brightly lit stage facing Marie. Comprehending the horror of it all, he froze as all the blood drained from his face. The announcer ran around the stage with his microphone commanding us all to *dance,* and the crowd got even more animated, cheering us on. Evidently Mr. Rugger then experienced a complete mental breakdown, for he started a strange new dance, hopping from one foot to the other as though his feet were either on fire or he was in imminent danger of not making it to a bathroom in time. Marie turned into a Japanese fan dancer and started waving her open hands in front of her face in a way suggesting she might be trying to disappear or change her identity. Mr. Lawrence, also in shock from having received a new fertility dance partner, became nearly apoplectic as he launched into his own version of the dance, which more closely resembled a tractor plow with a stuck steering mechanism, as he lurched around in circles. I continued moving my hips from side to side as I surreptitiously stepped backward toward the stairs, which I failed to see until I tripped and tumbled down them.

All dancing ceased and everyone on stage rushed over to help me. I was more embarrassed than hurt. My dress, which originally was slit to up my knee, was now slit to my waist. I repeatedly assured everyone I was going to be fine (once the body cast was removed), but Marie clung to me as though we were *both* in urgent need of medical assistance, or possibly a time machine, or better yet, a beaming device operated by a man named *Scotty* aboard the *Starship Enterprise.*

As soon as we could muster the dignity to do so, we hurriedly thanked anyone and everyone while waving and limping through the hotel back to the safety of our room.

Our next day in Hawaii had to be better than this, or we were going home.

DAY THREE: OUR KAYAK ADVENTURE

On the morning beginning the third day of our grand Hawaiian adventure, we decided to eat breakfast down in the hotel restaurant. We had noticed a sign outside the restaurant which read, *Free Continental Breakfast Available—See Within.* Upon entering the restaurant, we noticed a beautiful, sumptuous breakfast buffet in the center of the room, so without even looking at menus, we informed the hostess that we'd just be having the buffet. She smiled pleasantly and directed us to our table. We picked up our white china plates and headed to the long U-shaped table arrangement covered in crisp, white cloths and loaded with warming trays, pitchers and pots, and large silver platters and porcelain bowls, all filled with delicious breakfast choices. It was an artistic masterpiece of culinary delights. At the end of the long tables were cooktops, commandeered by two of the hotel's chefs, for immediate omelet preparations.

As we looked over the dishes attractively displayed, I grabbed Marie's arm and whispered into her ear, "Can you believe this, Marie? I mean, we've had pretty nice continental breakfasts before, but look at this! These people really know how to put on a spread for their hotel guests, huh?"

Marie smiled conspiratorially. "I think we know where we'll be eating breakfast from now on!"

We loaded up on powdered-sugar-dusted French toast, individually made omelets, smoked salmon with toasted bagels and cream cheese, hash browns, crisp bacon, fat little sausages, ripe strawberries, slices of pineapple, kiwi, and melon, yogurt, beautiful muffins and pastries, bite-sized cheesecake squares with fresh raspberries, assorted little boxes of cereal, buttery croissants, fresh-squeezed orange juice, and creamy hot chocolate. Of course we couldn't begin to eat everything on our plates, so we wrapped up our pastries, croissants, bagels, and bacon in paper napkins and dumped them in our beach bags, along with a few boxes of cereal. We stood and began to leave. Suddenly our friendly waitress vaulted across the dining room and stopped us.

"Excuse me, ladies, are you finished?" she asked, her smile a little thin.

"Why, yes we are, and thank you very much for that beautiful breakfast!" I quickly responded. "Wow, you sure provide your guests a fabulous spread here!"

"Well, thank you!" she answered sincerely. "Now did you want separate checks, or would you like this charged to your rooms?"

We stared at her and then at each other, as the reality of our situation settled in.

"You mean this *isn't* complimentary?" I asked.

Our waitress suppressed a laugh as she replied, "This?" She waved her hand toward the buffet. "No, *this* is not complimentary." She shook her head, emphasizing the point.

"Well, the sign said *Free Continental Breakfast,* right over there." I gestured toward the lobby.

The waitress pointed to a small table along the opposite wall of the restaurant on which stood a portable hot water dispenser with coffee and tea bags, juice boxes, a pitcher of milk, along with stacks of foam cups. Next to that was a tray containing foam plates and cereal bowls, plastic spoons and several packages of instant oatmeal and miniature boxes of Cheerios. Beside the cereal was a loaf of bread and a toaster with small packets of jam, jelly, and honey piled in a cardboard container. At the end of the table was a bowl filled with apples and bananas.

"*That* is the *free* continental breakfast buffet," she said.

"Separate checks, please," Marie responded quietly. We sat down and waited as our waitress prepared our bills.

She handed them to us with a little flourish and a final, "Thank you. Have a lovely day."

We stared at our bills.

"I think I'm going to be ill," I said.

"Do you think if we gave them back the stuff in our bags they'd reduce the bill?" Marie asked anxiously.

"No, I don't think so," I replied glumly. "We should have known this was too good to be true."

We paid sixty-five dollars apiece for our breakfast that day and learned a very valuable lesson in the process. Never order the breakfast buffet unless you are with a group of friends, and then order only one breakfast buffet and share it.

Marie and I grabbed a few apples on our way out. This breakfast cost us our food allowance for the entire day. The leftovers in our bags had to carry us through. At the rate we were spending money on food in this place, we'd be living out the last days of our Hawaiian vacation scrounging free sugar packets and complimentary after dinner mints.

We placed all our remaining breakfast items in the small fridge in our room and then headed downstairs for an attempt at having a pleasant, relaxing day on the island. We dressed a little smarter this time, wearing loose shorts and T-shirts over our swimming suits. We had towels in our bags and comfortable flip-flops on our feet. Clearly, we were getting a better feel for "island life."

As we walked through the lobby, Natalie, our favorite hotel activity leader, came bounding across the room, eagerly summoning us.

"Oh, Kay! Marie! There you are! Good morning! Mahalo! Are you ready to go have some fun? We have a wonderful activity planned for you today!"

"Um, Hi Natalie," I began. "We were thinking of just doing a little exploring today… "

"Well that's perfect!" She was giddy with excitement. "Come with me, you two! Exploring the island is exactly what we have planned for you today! We will be traveling along the beautiful Hule'ia River and then taking a short hike along the most pristine, gorgeous nature trail you have ever seen to some amazing waterfalls and natural clear, freshwater ponds for swimming. Lunch will be provided, of course." She smiled blissfully as though reliving her wedding night, and she wasn't even married.

"Hey, Kay, did you hear that? We get free lunch," Marie whispered as she poked me in my side with her sharp, bony elbow.

"I don't know, Marie…" I glanced nervously at Natalie, who jumped right back in.

"And look! You're both dressed perfectly for it too! You gals are all ready to go! Follow me! Your chariot awaits!" This girl could sell China to the Chinese.

We trooped along behind Natalie outside the hotel where there were several kayaks lined up along the length of the terrace. We also noticed a number of familiar faces among the other hotel guests who apparently had also been dragged into this.

"Those aren't chariots," Marie whispered nervously as she pointed to the kayaks.

"Here we are," Natalie chirped. "This is where the fun begins! Y'all get to kayak on the river to the nature trail where we begin our hike!"

She saw our hesitation after spotting the kayaks. I eyed our chirpy activity director suspiciously.

"Umm Natalie, we don't really know *how* to kayak. Maybe this isn't such a good idea…" I began.

"Oh, not to worry!" Natalie quickly interjected. "Kayaking is fun and very easy to do. Plus, these kayaks are all built for two! Since both of you will be paddling one kayak together, it takes very little effort. The river current will carry you all the way. You will love it, and we are even having a little practice drill right here before we head for the river. You'll see how easy it is. This is one Hawaiian adventure you don't want to miss!"

Natalie was wasted as a hotel activity director. She should have been a hostage negotiator for the PLO (Palestinian Liberation Organization).

Marie and I followed Natalie over to one of the kayaks, and we each took a seat. Marie sat in the front and I climbed in the back. We were handed paddles and shown how to paddle as a team. It did seem very easy, so we felt a little less nervous until we arrived at the river and had to put on hard helmets and heavy duty life vests. We all obediently stepped to the edge of the river and climbed into our kayaks. Josh, one of the kayak instructors, and his assistant, Chip, strapped us in. We recognized Lola and Joan, the hockey T-shirt girls; and C.J. and Spike with their soccer moms; and the two senior guys, Ezra and Vern, from the volleyball tournament, among others all getting into kayaks too. We were smiling and waving at each other as we got settled in the boats. Conspicuously missing from the group were Mr. Stanley Lawrence and his friend, Mr. Rugger. I sighed a little and wondered how they had managed to get out of this. Obviously they were more clever than we were. I wondered what they were up to on this beautiful day in Hawaii… probably on the beach relaxing, which is where I would be if I had a brain.

"Hey, Josh, what happens if this thing tips over while we're strapped in here?" Marie asked. "What do we do? Can we get out?" Marie sounded a little panicked, and truth to tell, so was I.

"Ladies, you have nothing to worry about. Just stay with the group. You won't tip over. These kayaks are designed to stay upright. Even if one of them did tip over, which is highly unlikely, it would flip topside again. That's the way they're built. Besides, this river is very slow moving and easy to navigate. Do just like we practiced and you'll be fine."

Josh and his assistant, Chip, eased our kayak out into the river, and we started paddling. At first we were right at the front of the pack. Occasionally we glanced back to see the others paddling along behind us. After a while I noticed our kayak starting to lag further and further behind the lead kayaks. Marie glanced back at me.

"I think we need to paddle a little harder, Kay. We're falling behind." We paddled harder.

Soon we were back up with the leaders. Ten minutes later however, we noticed several of our fellow kayakers moving up on our flanks. "Oh no! Look! I think they're going to pass us, Kay!" Marie turned and gave me an exasperated look.

"Hey, this isn't the Olympics here, Marie. So what if they pass us? Who cares?" I was starting to get more and more dumbfounded as our paddling seemed to become less and less effective and we failed to keep any kind of pace with the other kayaks on the river. Soon, all our kayaking companions were happily paddling further away into the distance.

"Aren't you paddling at all?" Marie called back in frustration.

"Hey, hello! I'm paddling like a maniac back here, Marie! My arms are ready to fall off! This boat just isn't moving! Could it be caught on something? I thought it was *you* who wasn't trying!"

Marie turned as far around as she could in her seat to look directly at me. "Well, if *you* are trying so *hard,* then why are you lying down?" she asked me in confusion.

Suddenly it occurred to me that I *was* practically lying down. The back of my seat seemed to have collapsed and as I struggled to lean against it for support, my body just gradually moved back right along with it until I was nearly flat on my back.

"It's the seat, Marie!" I cried. "There's something wrong with it!" I pulled myself up to a straight sitting position, unstrapped my seatbelt, and began tugging at the backrest of my seat to pull it upright. It wouldn't budge. "This seat is broken, Marie! I can't get it back up," I cried.

"Well, you'll just have to paddle without a seat back then, Kay! Come on, we've got to get moving! We're supposed to stay with the group, remember?" Marie waved her paddle in the air, indicating the last kayak, the one with ninety year olds Vern and Ezra, whose arms were about the size of broomsticks, smoothly paddling around a bend in the river a hundred yards ahead of us. I angrily strapped my seatbelt back on, and we began to paddle again.

After a few minutes I called out, "Hey, Marie! Would you please trade places with me for a while? My back is killing me!" Marie ignored me. A few minutes later I tried again. "Marie! I can't paddle without any back support! I'm dying back here! Can't you trade with me for just a little while?"

"No, I can't trade with you, Kay!" Marie yelled back at me. "We're not supposed to climb around in this thing. It will tip over. I'm sorry. We just have to keep going. Come on, Kay. You're so amazing! You can do this! Just *be* the paddle. *Be* the kayak rushing on the river! *Be* the river—"

"Hey, Marie," I interrupted. "You'll *be* on the next rocket to Mars if you don't shut up. We're just going to have to pull over and stop. I can't go on. Besides, we've been paddling forever on this stupid river! That idiot activities director Natalie said we'd only be doing this kayak thing for a little while! I swear I'm going to whack her to death with this useless, worthless paddle when we get back to the hotel."

I was miserable and completely exhausted. Marie was silent as we paddled over to the river's edge. Just as we were about to climb out, ditch our kayak, and start walking back to civilization, we saw Josh and Chip hailing us and rowing their kayak in our direction like a couple Olympians. Their sleek kayak flew through the water and before we knew it, they were pulling up beside us.

"Kay, Marie, thank goodness you're okay. We didn't realize you weren't with us until we started counting the boats at the stopping point. Why are you over here in the shallows? What's going on?" Josh was clearly concerned.

"Well, Josh," I began, "We are over here because we got stuck in a *defective* kayak. *That's* what's going on. The rear seat is broken. It collapsed on me!"

Josh maneuvered his kayak closer to ours and examined the seat. "Oh no," he muttered, "We knew there were problems with a few of these. Hey, check this out, Chip!"

Now I was upset. "You mean to tell me you knew some of your kayaks had problems? *Now* you tell us this?" I glowered at Josh.

"We thought we had them all repaired, but we must have missed this one," Josh responded apologetically.

It was at this point I made a *huge* error in judgment. My plan was to jump from the kayak to the shore so Josh could repair my seat without me in the way, but instead, the moment I stepped to the edge of the kayak, I tipped it off balance. It flipped over with Marie still strapped in her seat.

"Oh no!" I screamed, as I tumbled over, crashing into the water like a lumbering bear. I struggled to find my footing, stood up, and turned back to the kayak. For some reason our amazingly engineered kayak did not flip right back over as Josh had earlier assured us it *would.* Marie was trapped under there. For one horrifying moment, we were all frozen in time staring at the overturned kayak as it began to float away. But then, in the space of a heartbeat, Josh and Chip released their seat restraints, leaped into the water, and grabbed our kayak, flipping it right side up. Marie was sputtering and coughing. She snapped her head around and glared at me.

"What did you do *that* for," she shrieked. I could see steam rising from her dripping helmet.

"Oh gosh, Marie. I'm so sorry! Really I am. I was just trying to get out of the way so Josh could fix my seat… honestly! I didn't know it would do that. I'm sorry..." I finished lamely. I felt like a murderer. I practically drowned my best friend.

Josh reached over to Marie to steady and calm her.

"It's okay, Marie. You're okay. We're going to man both kayaks now. Our stopping point is right around that bend just ahead. Honestly, you were almost there! Kay, if you'd sit in my kayak with Chip here, he will paddle, and I will paddle from your seat in this one." Chip and Josh quickly moved into position after helping me into their kayak, and we moved smoothly over the water around the bend to where everybody waited for us on the shore. The moment our boats appeared, the crowd started clapping and cheering. It seemed we were getting clapped and cheered at a lot since coming to Hawaii. Marie and I waved and smiled a little bleakly as we pulled up to where the other kayaks were "collected."

"Oh, Josh," I called to him as I stepped out of the kayak, "just so you know, I'm never climbing into another one of these things again."

"Oh, no problem, Kay!" Josh was smiling broadly at me. "We'll be traveling back in a speed boat."

Why we didn't just *go* there in a speedboat to begin with was a mystery I'll never understand.

Even though Marie and I were soaking wet, the day was so warm and mild, we didn't feel cold, and our clothes dried quickly in the sun. We began the hiking portion of our journey. Amazingly, neither Marie nor I had lost our flip flops during Marie's near drowning episode, so we didn't have to hike barefoot; however, walking barefoot here would not have been a problem. The trail was blanketed with a soft, velvety carpet of leaves and warm, moist earth. The views were breathtaking, and the smells in the forest reminded me of late summer camping trips back home, only the vegetation here was more lush and beautiful. Natalie was right. This was a hike we would be sorry to have missed.

We stopped for lunch when we arrived at the falls. Josh and Chip unloaded a cooler they had carried up from a boat conveniently moored nearby. We had sandwiches, cold sodas, chips, and cookies. It all tasted perfectly wonderful. We sat, relaxed, and enjoyed the falls. Josh was a veritable encyclopedia of Hawaiian trivia. For example, we learned that there are *no* snakes on the island of Kauai, which was strictly okay with me, as I had an irrational fear of them. Still, I thought it a little improbable, and I started searching for any signs of snakes after that.

Soon it was announced that we would be hiking a little farther to the "pools" where we could all swim. We all eagerly followed Josh and Chip down the trail. The morning had slipped away and the sun was now directly overhead. It was plenty warm, and we were ready for a cool dip.

Suddenly we entered a beautiful grotto hidden by lush foliage, with a wide, deep natural pool fed by a series of pleasant waterfalls. Rising from the bank near the edge of the pond was a sturdy tree and from one of the limbs hung a rope swing. Apparently the swing was our way into the pool. Marie and I looked at the swing and then at each other dubiously. We were a little beyond the age of swinging from ropes. Actually, neither of us had ever swung from a rope for any reason, and we weren't eager to start now. There was a big knot tied at the bottom which was supposed to be sort of a seat you straddled as you hung on. Then Josh or Chip would pull the swing with pond-bound volunteer attached, all the way back, and release it. Once the swing was well over the water, the person hanging on simply let go and dropped into the pool. Both Josh and Chip took a turn demonstrating how to hold onto and let go of the rope. Josh did a simple drop into the pool that made it look easy. But as Chip swung out over the water, he hiked his legs up over his head and performed a flip into the water. Everyone oohed and aahed and a few said the somersault looked like more fun… *well, good luck with that, guys.* Josh and Chip swam to the edge of the pond and jogged back up the bank like a couple sure-footed mountain goats to begin assisting us as we lined up for a turn at the swing. I had begun searching for another way into the pool, but there were no "trails" down to the water, and the descent to the pond from where we stood looked very rocky, mossy, and slippery. One by one, members of our group swung out over the water and dropped in. Marie and I kept moving to the end of the line, but eventually, we were the only ones left. I bravely stepped forward.

I straddled the big knot at the base of the swing and hung on to the rope for dear life. Josh pulled the swing back and let go. My heart did a dozen flip-flops as the rope swung out over the water but then, thankfully, it swung right back to Josh's waiting hands.

As Josh caught the rope, I said, "Whew! Wow! Well, *that* was fun!"

I started to climb off the swing. Josh steadied me and said, "No, Kay, you're supposed to *let go* of the rope and drop *into the water.*"

"Oh yeah, I forgot that part," I mumbled. "When exactly am I supposed to let go again?"

"Tell you what," Josh said patiently, "I'll call out the words '*let go*' when it's time and when you hear that, just let go, okay?"

"Okay." My voice was shaky and so were my nerves. All of a sudden the pool looked like a deep, dark well of death into which I was going to get sucked and never return.

Once again Josh pulled me back and let the swing go. Predictably, he shouted "Let go!"

I instantly obeyed and clumsily fell in the direction of the water, but I never arrived there. Somehow my foot got tangled up in the rope and I was now dangling upside down. When the rope swung back towards my cohorts standing along the edge of the river, my head banged into the bank. I could hear both Josh and Chip scramble toward the rope, which was now beginning to veer away from them. First I heard Josh yelling, "Get it, Chip! Can you reach it? Grab her!" Chip missed the "grab." Then I heard Marie, in her best cheerleading voice, shouting out, "Get Kay! Get the rope! Get it! Get it!" Memories of a thousand missed volleyball passes with Marie jumping up and down yelling those very same words came rushing into my mind as I swayed away from the bank and their reaching hands.

"Well, there she goes," Vern called out helpfully from where he was floating down in the water.

As the rope swung the second time over the water, I tried to hoist myself up and get untangled, but I was unable to do it before the rope returned to the shore. My hip and free leg crashed into the bank. Chip, Josh, and Marie all lunged for me. This time they caught me and pulled me securely to shore. Soon I was untangled and standing with Marie on the bank, feeling like a total fool.

"Gee guys, all this *fun* and *free lunch* too." I shot Marie a withering glance. I watched Josh and Chip with trepidation as they checked the swing and tied up the excess rope fringe dangling beneath the knot, so it wouldn't hang up anyone else.

"All right, Kay, I'm going with you this time, okay?" Josh took my hand and gently tugged. I didn't move.

"Just how exactly are you going to 'go with me,' Josh?" I asked nervously.

"Well, Kay, I'm going to straddle this big knot in the swing, and you are going to straddle me. We'll go together. Is that okay?"

This was the best offer from a good looking guy I'd had in some time, so I complied. Over the water Josh and I went. We dropped together into the water, only somewhere from the rope to the water, I fell away from Josh and managed to land flat on my back, with a resounding slap on the water. I don't think I went more than two inches beneath the surface. I just lay on top of the water with my back stinging. I could see Marie cheering and jumping up and down on the bank. I tried to smile and wave at her, but

I was having a little trouble breathing. I noticed the water was quite chilly, but I couldn't think beyond that. Suddenly Josh had me. He wrapped his strong arms around my shoulders and pulled me away from the drop zone. Boy, oh boy, I could get used to this. Too bad Josh was the same age as my daughter, Susan. Actually, if this kid didn't have any ambitions beyond kayaking down rivers and swinging from ropes, I could definitely picture Suzi going for him in a big way.

Now it was Marie's turn. Marie sailed out over the water and let go of the rope at the perfect moment, entering the water feet first like a pro. I really hated that girl sometimes.

As fun as paddling around a natural pool of water looks, it's really not that fun. The water tends to be cold, deep, and sort of creepy. Once all the hotel guests were safely in the pool, Chip joined us and we all splashed and swam, and when we got a little tired, we floated on our backs, gazing up through the trees. Then Josh and Chip showed us how to get out of the pond, which was tricky business. Fortunately, we had been given "water" shoes, which were similar to thin tennis shoes and equipped with heavily ribbed soles to give us some traction while climbing on the slippery rocks surrounding the pool. Marie and I hung onto each other as we ponderously picked our way over the rocks and back up the river bank. We were exhausted, our hair and makeup ruined, and our freshly manicured nails looked atrocious.

We nearly froze to death on the boat ride back to civilization. Our driver was another teenage kid named—

and I'm not kidding about this—*Speed.* Speed lived up to his name by driving the boat as though trying to outrun enemy gunships. We got thoroughly soaked with the spray. The wind had also come up, making the whole experience utterly miserable. We were starting to believe this whole travel/adventure business was nothing like what was being experienced by all of those eager, ecstatically happy vacationers snorkeling, scuba diving, sailing, riding jet skis, and relaxing with cool drinks on the travel channel. So far we hadn't gotten any of that. Well... tomorrow was another day.

DAY FOUR: SNORKELING FOR LOVERS

When we arrived back at the hotel from our kayak adventure, we hurried to our room where we relaxed in the warmth of our Jacuzzi tub for a solid hour, allowing the water jets to massage and relax all our sore muscles. Following that, we showered, climbed into our pajamas, and watched an old Cary Grant movie on cable television while picnicking on our leftovers from breakfast. We opened our windows and sliding glass doors so we could see and hear the ocean. We went outside to sit at the little table on our private deck, where we played several hands of our favorite card game, gin rummy. Following that, we watched the sun set. It was a perfect ending to a less-than-perfect day.

We woke early the following morning with a plan. After hurriedly dressing in beach-combing clothes, we snuck out of the hotel into the misty, pre-dawn morning. We strolled along the beach looking for shells, starfish, pretty rocks, and sand dollars, but the beach seemed to have been swept clean during the night, which was okay too. The morning air was misty and cool but before long, we had to pull off our light jackets and tie the arms around our waists to keep from getting too warm. We walked and talked and frequently stopped just to look out to sea and watch the waves roll in. The scene before us was perfectly perfect, and we were excited to finally be embarking upon a day of whatever we pleased, free from activity directors and their preplanned island pursuits.

When we returned to the hotel, we avoided the lobby and found some stairs leading to the second level where we stepped onto the elevator and took it up to our floor. We changed into our swimsuits and covered them with loose shorts and T-shirts. We threw towels into our beach bags along with suntan lotion, sunglasses, light zip-up jackets, a reasonable amount of spending money, and water bottles. We managed to get out of the hotel without either Natalie or Nicole, our activity directors, noticing.

Instead of immediately returning to the beach, we decided to wander along the streets, looking in shops and checking out the local culture.

Our lovely Hawaiian island was not really that "happening" of a place early in the morning—but then, besides Las Vegas and New York, what place is? Well maybe Hong Kong, but only because it is so crowded, the people who live there have to sleep in shifts. But here in Kauai, there were very few people walking about, and it was still too early for the shops to be open. Eventually the scent of fresh baked bread led us to an attractive little corner café that was open, so we decided to try it out. The menu offered a good variety of breakfast choices, but they were all way out of our price range. We concluded that if we shared the cheapest item on the menu, we could afford a plain toasted bagel for five dollars and ninety-nine cents.

"Gee, they don't really have any great breakfast specials here like Denny's, do they?" Marie asked.

"No, they sure don't." I sighed. Even sharing one breakfast order cost us more than our food budget allowed. We split a twenty dollar breakfast *special,* which consisted of a cheese omelet, toast, hash browns, and a glass of juice.

After breakfast, we continued walking along the street where several of the shops were beginning to open, so we ventured into a few of them. I found a cute pair of flip-flops, an island T-shirt, and matching visor. Then I splurged on a pair of tortoiseshell earrings, carved to look like seabirds in flight. I thought them beautiful. I even thought myself rather beautiful when I put them on, but I wasn't. My face, which was a little thin and long already, took on the proportions of a primitive Greek horse with these dangling appendages hanging from my earlobes. Marie purchased a beautiful, framed Hawaiian painting. The image on the canvas was of two children running in the surf with a colorful kite. Two adults watched them from beach chairs under a bright umbrella. There were sails out on the water and gulls soaring in the air. It was a pleasant, happy summertime picture.

We continued meandering along, stopping to browse in several shops. Soon we were laden with packages, and there was nothing to do but return to the hotel and deposit them in our room. We planned to spend the rest of the day relaxing on the beach. As luck would have it, just as we came around the corner leading to the bank of hotel elevators, Natalie spotted us. We hurried into the nearest elevator and started punching every button on the wall, but we were too slow. Natalie's hand snaked through the door just as it was closing, and she jammed the elevator door back open.

"Hey, you two! I wondered where you had gone off to! I see you went shopping! How fun! Oh my gosh, you should have come to me! I know where all the best stores are! Don't you just love the shops around here? What did you buy? Do you mind showing me?" Natalie was practically drooling with curiosity and excitement.

She grabbed my hand and looped her arm through Marie's and pulled us away from our escape, back into the lobby. We showed her the things we had purchased, and she fell all over herself with joy and happiness, followed by copious amounts of praise over our selections. Much as I wanted to run away from Natalie, there was something very endearing about her.

"You did hear about the snorkeling outing planned for today, didn't you?" Natalie looked into our faces anxiously, as though the fate of the world rested upon our response.

"Well, Natalie, actually we hadn't," I replied.

"Well, thank goodness I caught you in time," she exclaimed.

As one, Marie and I took one step backward. This time we were going to hold our ground. Every activity Natalie had dragged us into had been a disaster.

"No, Natalie," Marie spoke firmly. "You are darling, and it sounds like a lot of fun, but we just plan to spend the day relaxing on the beach. Thanks anyway though."

Marie smiled her sweetest smile and linked her arm in mine. As we started to turn back to the elevators, Nicole, our other activity director banged through one of the hotel entrances and charged into the lobby with a group of eight to ten people trooping along behind her. Marie froze. Her eyes locked onto the tallest figure in the group. My eyes followed hers, and there he was. Spying us at the same moment, Mr. Rugger began striding purposely toward us with a big smile on his face, his eyes fixed on Marie.

Marie quickly found her voice. "Or, we could join *you,* Natalie, and do something a whole lot more fun than just lying on the beach!"

Natalie smiled happily and clapped her hands. "Oh, thank goodness! You changed your mind! I'm so glad! You are just going to love this! Snorkeling is the most fun ever! You'll see!"

Marie virtually *wafted* across the floor to Mr. Rugger, leaving me standing alone holding all our packages. Stanley Lawrence was nowhere to be seen. Natalie turned back to me.

"Um, wait a minute, Natalie." I stopped her before she could grab me and drag me into the group. "Look, I have to take all these packages up to our room, and honestly, I'm not feeling up to it. I think I'll take a pass on the activity this time, okay? I'm sorry but... good news! Marie will be going!"

Natalie's face was a mask of confusion and disappointment as I turned back to the bank of elevators. Just as I leaned in to push the *up* arrow, the elevator opened. There stood Mr. Stanley Lawrence. His eyes opened wide and a big smile spread over his face.

"Well, what do you know? Kay Taylor—just the person I was looking for! I hope you're joining our snorkeling excursion today."

He stepped from the elevator and pulled a few of the larger packages out of my arms. Oh, I loved when a man did that... unless of course the man was more of the not-so-nice-after-all-robber type guy who dropped *out* of boy scouts before earning the *helpful neighbor* merit badge. I glanced back over at our perky activity director, whose confused expression was turning to one of bemusement.

"Or," I said, looking straight at Natalie, "I could join *you,* and do something a whole lot more fun than just resting in my room!"

Natalie was watching us with a satisfied little smile on her face. This girl was no dummy. Natalie signaled a bellman, who carried all of Marie's and my packages to our room.

Activity group complete, we were all ushered outside to the terrace where a mountain of snorkeling equipment was stacked. Standing beside this heap of gear and looking somewhat official were our Kayaking leaders, Josh and Chip. Josh wasted no time greeting us and then he launched in, giving us a brief lesson on the equipment and how to properly use it, including *spitting* into the mask to help keep it clear. We all tried on the face gear, which made us look like aliens, and we then put the flippers on our feet, which made us resemble duck-footed, goose-stepping Nazi aliens. This strange rubberized *attire* had to look better in the water. We flipper-slapped our way to the hotel swimming pool where we practiced using our gear in the water.

Snorkeling rehearsal over, we headed to the hotel vans and were driven to an area of beach, off of which resided a significant reef—home to an enormous variety of tropical fish. We re-dressed ourselves in our snorkeling equipment and stomped into the surf. Most of us immediately fell over the moment we tried to walk in the ocean.

Evidently Marie and I entered the ocean at a particularly turbulent spot because we both began to be buffeted by the incoming waves. We bounced around like corks in a storm. Within moments, Stanley had come to my rescue, and Jim had pulled Marie to her feet. Josh and Chip had also splashed over and guided the four of us beyond the breaking waves into deeper water. We had to re-situate our masks which were now hanging around our necks and which took an inordinate amount of time to reposition. Eventually we were ready to actually begin snorkeling, which nearly all of our companions had already been doing for some time. We pressed our faces into the water, kicked with our flippers, and began to look around.

I was immediately transported into the most amazing martian landscape I had ever seen. The colors were magnificent. The reef itself was spectacular, and an incredible array of aquatic creatures scuttled, fluttered, and glided in every direction beneath us!

We found ourselves surrounded by a thousand shimmering delicate fish in breathtakingly vivid colors. There were spotted fish, striped fish, iridescent, and speckled fish—some with flowing gossamer tails, others with bowl-shaped, paper-thin bodies. They scooted and bobbed, darted and danced. After several minutes, I looked from side to side for my companions, but there didn't appear to be any people swimming near me. I lifted my head and looked out over the surface of the water. Our snorkeling group was scattered everywhere. In seconds I found Marie, but she was happily paddling away with Mr. Rugger. Then I saw Stan swimming toward me. I submerged to look at his face underwater. At first he gave me a little wave with his fingers, but then he reached for my hand so we could stay together. He started pointing toward a colorful school of fish a short distance away. I nodded vigorously, and we kicked over to where they were. We tried to touch the fish, which appeared to be right beneath us. But I soon discovered that no matter how hard I tried, I couldn't reach the fish to touch them, which told me that when looking underwater, my depth perception was completely non-operational. We continued holding hands, which I found almost as exciting as all the beautiful fish surrounding us.

After a while I began noticing the water becoming shallower and the fish more scarce. We could almost kneel on the ocean floor here. I was just about to lift my head from the water to see where in the world we were when Stan pointed to something moving swiftly in the rocks. Suddenly a large snake seemed to leap out from the depths and slither right toward me. Immediately I reacted. I pulled away from Stan and literally went berserk, kicking, splashing, screaming, and lunging away from the dangerous ocean creature. In the midst of this maelstrom, it never occurred to me that I could easily stand up right where I was, but I couldn't think beyond my terror. I cut my hands and knees on the sharp rocks beneath me in my frenzied attempts to escape. Suddenly, Stan grabbed me around my waist and pulled me to my feet. He hugged me close and smoothly eased me away from the snake-infested area. We had somehow snorkeled onto a sandbar, which was a great distance from the shore. This also unnerved me but at that moment, I was safe. I was in the arms of a very attractive, very sexy man. Even though I knew I was out of danger, I was shaking uncontrollably.

Stan pulled off his mask and began speaking gently into my ear. "Calm down, Kay. I've got you. It's okay. There's nothing to be afraid of. You're safe." At that moment I started to cry, and my cries turned into sobs, which I couldn't seem to control. Stan gently rubbed my shoulders and back until I was calm.

There was a strip of dry beach atop this sandbar, which seemed very strange to me, as we were very far from shore. It was like a tiny desert island. Stan pulled off his flippers and tossed them onto the dry area, then swept me up in his arms and carried me to our private little beach, where we both sat down.

"Are you okay?" he asked. Our masks were off, and there was an indescribable intensity in his eyes as he studied my face.

"They told us there weren't any snakes in Kauai," I stated flatly.

"That wasn't a snake, Kay. It was an eel—scary looking, but quite harmless actually."

"Well, it didn't look harmless to me," I responded bitterly.

We sat in silence. Stan continued to watch me carefully, waiting…waiting. My emotions were too close. More tears began to gather in the corners of my eyes and slid down my face. And that was when I told Mr. Stanley Lawrence all about Neil. I spoke of my longing and loneliness, my sadness and regret. I told him about how good, responsible, and companionable Neil had been.

And that was when Stan told me all about his wife, Janice—how warm, vibrant, and talented she had been. Janice had been taken too soon, like my Neil. We had that common bond. Providence had opened a window of opportunity, and we were able to share all our protected, private grief. And, as we did so, we experienced true healing from those overwhelming losses.

We sat quietly together for a long time after that. Stan gently took my hands and kissed the cuts on my palms. Then he kissed the cuts on my knees. All the while, his eyes never left mine. It was the most erotic thing I'd ever experienced.

After a period of time, which neither of us could approximate with any degree of accuracy, we heard a speedboat. It was approaching rapidly, and I could see Marie jumping up and down in the boat, waving and anxiously calling out, "There they are! There! Right over here! Kay! Kay, we're coming! Hold on! We're coming! Don't move!" I smiled and waved. At that moment, I was perfectly happy and all was right with the world.

The boat stopped several hundred feet from where we were because of the sandbar, and the pilot waved us over. Stan helped me to my feet and while carrying our gear, we awkwardly made our way to the boat. Jim and Marie helped us climb onboard.

"Thank goodness you're all right!" Marie cried. "We were so worried. We all showed up at the pier at eleven, but you weren't there. We thought you had drowned or been kidnapped by pirates or something!"

Marie was nothing if not dramatic.

"No, we just got sidetracked," I responded calmly.

Marie glanced at me and then at Stan, and back at me again. A smile began to spread across her features.

"They got sidetracked," she repeated to Jim, whose expression of concern had also been replaced with a goofy grin. The engine of the boat roared to life, and we were quickly transported to the dock. Josh and Chip were waiting to collect our snorkeling gear. We gathered our clothing and bags and made our way up the beach toward our hotel. It appeared we had a whole afternoon in front of us with no particular plans. Marie and I glanced at each other as we approached the hotel entrance. Neither Jim nor Stan had said anything about continuing on together, and we were too old fashioned to jump in there with any suggestions of our own. Fortunately, Jim broke the ice.

"So, would you girls allow us to take you somewhere really amazing for lunch?"

Without hesitation we both nodded in the affirmative and the matter was settled. Apparently, on the day Marie and I were paddling our defective kayak to the pools of doom, Stan and Jim had been exploring the island.

We climbed into the guys' rental car, a silver BMW, which was about a million times nicer than our metallic-green Ford Fiesta.

We relaxed in the plush leather seats of the BMW and traveled in luxury to a large sugarcane plantation, which, in its heyday, had been owned by the very wealthy *Lord Somebody Or Other* from England. The main house was now a restaurant. We received a delightful old-fashioned horse and buggy ride all over the property and the driver, clad in an authentic 1800s livery costume, told us all sorts of interesting historical tidbits about the house and plantation. The grounds were beautiful and to make the setting complete, a number of stately peacocks strutted confidently around the yards and gardens. We received a lesson on how sugarcane was harvested. Apparently it took a *whole* lot of sugarcane to make a small amount of sugar. I was reminded of cooking spinach leaves at home and how quickly all those leaves would reduce to a tiny little mound after being heated on the stove. After the tour we headed into the main house for lunch. We ordered a seafood platter and shared it. During lunch Marie giggled a lot, and Stan and I stole frequent glances at each other. After sharing so many intimate details about our private lives, we both felt a little awkward. Fortunately, Jim was in a talkative mood, and he filled all the silences, regaling us with story after story. Later on, both Stan and Jim enlightened us about the ins and outs of owning a sports supply company in Phoenix, Arizona. Evidently they had quite a large number of stores they supplied sporting goods *to.* They were working on increasing their Hawaiian market and planned to finalize a deal the following afternoon with a Mr. Kamuela, the head of a sportswear company on Kauai. After their meeting with Mr. Kamuela, they were planning to leave the island in order to meet with another sportswear company the day after that on the island of Maui. When this information surfaced, I couldn't help notice Marie's face fall a little. The realization that this wonderful romance we were experiencing was probably nothing more than a "fling" for these guys made us both feel a little sad.

After lunch, Marie and I were shown more of the island, including a beautiful nature preserve that looked vaguely familiar. We decided to omit our story of getting lost and stuck, probably in that very same nature preserve after our arrival on the island. The shadows lengthened as we drove along, marveling at the scenery, and talking together. In what seemed like an unbelievably short period of time, we had wound our way around the entire island and were being deposited at the front door of our hotel. Just as Marie started to step away from Jim onto the curb, he reached out and took her arm.

"Would you like to do something with us tomorrow?" he asked.

Marie's face lit up like a Christmas tree. "What do you have in mind?" She glanced at him, then over at Stan. The two men appeared to be exchanging some sort of cryptic visual signals.

"Well, we were thinking of trying the Waimea Canyon Bicycle downhill ride. Are you girls game?"

"I think I can remember how to ride a bike. What do you think, Kay?"

"Well, I don't know. I was planning to stay here and study the migrating habits of sponges."

Stan laughed. "Well, LORD knows it's hard to compete with *a sponge.* What if we sweetened the deal with lunch?"

"Where do we meet and when?"

"How about right here tomorrow morning around seven thirty?"

"It's a date," I replied enthusiastically. "Guess we'll see you then!"

We hurried to the elevators. Once we were safely inside our suite, we danced around giggling like schoolgirls. We called room service and ordered lobster dinners, which we thoroughly enjoyed on our deck while watching the sun disappear in a fireball of liquid golden magenta.

We spent a quiet evening in our room discussing the events of the day. As it turned out, and to no one's surprise, Marie had fallen hard for Jim Rugger and predictably, I was terribly worried about her being hurt by him. But what worried me even more was what I was feeling for Mr. Stanley Lawrence. What was happening to us? Here we were, footloose and fancy free, on our first real adventure, and we were falling headlong in *love* with the first two available men to come along! It could have been pretty wonderful, except in two days, it would all be over.

DAY FIVE: DEATH BY BICYCLE

Marie and I stood out on our deck watching a dark, dense fog roll in from the ocean as the fifth day of our vacation dawned on Kauai.

"What do you think, Marie? Do you suppose the guys are still going to want to bicycle down a winding canyon road in this?" I squinted, trying to see farther into the distance. If not for the sound of the waves crashing on the shore, there was no evidence of an ocean anywhere, or anything else for that matter.

"Well, it's nearly seven thirty." Marie sighed. "The guys will be waiting. We better get downstairs."

We headed to the street, but it wasn't until we nearly fell off the curb that we saw Stan and Jim's rental car waiting there.

"Hey, Kay!" Stan was practically hanging out the window. "Are you girls ready to go?"

"*Are* we still going?" I asked uncertainly.

"Of course! This fog will blow off, and we'll have a perfectly fine day to bicycle in! Come on. You'll see! It'll be great!" All of a sudden, Stan sounded a *whole* lot like our activity director, Natalie, which was a little alarming. Evidently the bicycle plan was still on. Stan and Jim jumped out of the car and came around to let us in. Marie and I glanced at each other anxiously.

"Death by bicycle," Marie whispered to me.

"At least we're wearing new underwear." I responded quietly, as we climbed in the car.

This had all the earmarks of certain, unavoidable disaster. I strained to see out the window of the car. We drove to a bicycle outfitter shop where we signed some sort of legal paper, releasing the bicycle company from any responsibility or liability should any of us accidentally drive one of their bikes off a cliff or into a volcano or something. We all stated that we were of sound mind and body (well… this was one of those debatables) and also that we knew how to ride a bicycle. We stood around the bicycle shop as several additional enthusiastic bicycle-riding tourists wandered in to join the canyon downhill ride. Soon everyone was outfitted for the bicycle ride. We all jumped into a big van, upon which all the bicycles were loaded. We were slowly and carefully driven through the fog to the top of Waimea Canyon, which is about thirty-five hundred feet above sea level. Evidently the bicycle shop owner cared more about the forty dollars per head he collected from us than our lives. We were given elaborate safety instructions and helmets, like they would help once we were plummeting through the air toward the bottom of this canyon. We were all given bicycles, which were adjusted to our sizes and told to pedal around a little at the top of the hill to get comfortable riding them. The fog was a little thinner up here, but the visibility was still pretty poor. We rode our bicycles around a pullout area at the summit, and on our second time around, I accidentally veered into Marie. Fortunately we were moving at such a slow pace, we were able to simply step from the pedals to the ground to keep from falling over.

"Sorry, Marie. Am I the only person who thinks riding a bike down a mountain road in fog is insane?"

Marie looked over at me as she adjusted her helmet. "I think we're all crazy. Did you see the road we drove on to get up here? It is full of hairpin turns and has a bunch of scary-looking drop-offs. I bet our activity directors back at the hotel had something safer planned, like bungee jumping into a volcano. Where are they when you really need them?"

We both looked over at Stan and Jim, who were alternating practicing wheelies and seeing who could balance the longest standing on their pedals while holding their bikes motionless, followed by maniacally twisting their front tires from side to side, trying to knock each other off balance.

"Who are those guys?" Marie asked.

"Well Marie, yesterday *those guys* were two semi-rational adult males with jobs, mothers, stock brokers, and occasional flashes of marginal intelligence, but today… I have no idea."

"Bizarro world?" Marie conjectured.

"Exactly." I sidled my bike closer to Marie's and we watched the guys one-up each other like juvenile delinquents.

After several minutes we were all called over to begin our bicycle descent and reminded once yet again how to navigate from the turnoff at the bottom of the canyon to the coastal road (you can't miss it) leading to a large park where we were all to meet for lunch. While Stan and Jim whipped to the front of the group as though preparing to take on the Tour de France, Marie and I settled in at the back of the pack. We were all given the "go ahead," and Jim and Stan immediately disappeared into the mist. Marie and I eased our bikes along the center of the road, riding the brakes at a snail's pace for the first mile of the descent. After a period of time, we noticed that we were the only two bicyclists crawling along the middle of the road, hugging the center line. Everyone else had moved to the far right-hand side and had proceeded more confidently into the distance. A large town car suddenly appeared, looming toward us around a curve, and the driver laid on his horn. Marie and I both veered crazily away from the center line. My bicycle ran directly into the guardrail on the shoulder of the road, and Marie crashed her bicycle right into the back of mine. We both fell hard with our bikes to the ground.

"Ouch! Oh gosh, Kay, help! Owww! Oh, no! I think I twisted my foot! Are you okay?" Marie was hopping on one foot as she attempted to pull her bicycle upright.

"Oh my heck! *No,* Marie, I'm *not* all right. Did you have to run into me? Now I've scraped my hands and knees again! Holy mother, that stings!"

"Well, I think I cracked my pubic bone when I fell on that dopey bicycle bar!" Marie was now sort of crouching as she hopped around on one foot.

"Geez, that really hurts, Kay! What if I fractured myself down there or something? Oh, my poor kids!" Marie wailed. (Like her kids had anything to do with this.) Marie continued miserably. "How come they don't give the girls *girl* bikes to ride?"

We both hobbled around a bit and finally realized we were probably going to live, but scrapes, bumps, and bangs *hurt,* and we were both in real discomfort as we carefully rolled our bicycles back onto the road.

"At least our bikes are all right," Marie muttered.

"This is all *their* fault, Marie," I snapped, referring to our "dates."

"First they drag us up here, and then they *abandon* us! Why do we keep saying 'yes' to these insane activities anyway?"

Marie continued gingerly putting weight on her hurt foot, easing it up and down and from side to side.

"I think my foot's okay. I just twisted it a little when I fell, but that seat's gonna hurt to sit on. We better get going, Kay. Everybody else is way ahead of us now!" Marie gestured down the road, which was, at this point in time, eerily quiet. The rest of the group was long gone. The good news was that the fog had cleared, just as predicted. Now that we could see more clearly, we were transported by the beauty of the scenes opening before us. We rode our bikes more gingerly, taking plenty of time to enjoy the panoramic views of the ocean, which appeared after every curve in the road, like a bright, vivid snapshot. We stopped several times to just look out at it in amazement.

"The views up here are spectacular aren't they?" Marie said as we stood beside our bicycles transfixed by the splendor of the canyon and ocean beyond.

"Yeah, I'll say! This is amazing! Hey, Marie, I wonder where the guys are."

Suddenly, as if on cue, Jim and Stan appeared, pumping their bicycles for all they were worth toward us.

"Hey Marie… Kay!" Jim called out. "Thank good… goodness… you're o… okay!

Where'd you… where'd… you go?" Jim was panting as he pedaled over to Marie.

"We didn't go anywhere, Jim. You're the ones who took off like your shirts were on fire!" Marie waited as Jim struggled to catch his breath.

Stan, dripping with sweat, was also struggling to speak.

"Sor… sorry… about… that," he managed as he reached out for my hand. "What's this?" He looked more closely at my hands. "These scrapes are fresh. Did you fall?"

"Well, yeah, sort of. We had a little wreck on our bikes," I responded. "But no permanent damage done." I looked into his concerned expression and those luscious blue eyes, and I knew I was a goner.

"Yeah, we had a little altercation with the guard rail when some crazy driver ran us off the road!" Marie exclaimed.

"Was it that black town car?" Jim asked anxiously. "We noticed it go past. The driver should have slowed down! What an idiot." Jim shook his head in disgust. "Sorry we weren't here to help you. We just figured you were right behind us... Sorry."

Their breathing was returning to normal. "Man, it sure is a whole lot easier going down than coming up!" Jim wiped the perspiration from his face with the sleeve of his shirt. "I'm glad you guys weren't farther up the road than this! I don't know if we could have pushed ourselves much farther!"

"Well, we're glad you came back... Thank you." Marie smiled up at Jim with undisguised adoration.

Stan was watching me with just a hint of a smile. My stomach did a dozen flip-flops. Suddenly my knees and hands didn't hurt nearly as much anymore, and Marie's hobble had disappeared. We climbed back on our bicycles and coasted together to the bottom of the canyon.

As we emerged from the canyon, Marie and I pulled up behind Jim and Stan, expecting them to simply continue leading us to the meeting place where the other cyclists and lunch waited. They glanced a little uncertainly back at us and then at each other.

"Hey Jim, do you remember what that kid said about where we were supposed to go once we got down here?" Stan asked casually.

Jim squinted and looked up and down the road, which branched off in three different directions. "Well, Stan my man, I remember him saying something about a park and a coastal highway, but all three of these roads look pretty coastal to me. I don't see any coastal road signs or any parks for that matter. Hmmm. Let's go right and see where it takes us. Come on, girls. It's this way!" Jim called out confidently.

Marie looked worried. "Oh, oh, Kay. Did you hear that?" Marie whispered as she edged closer to me. "Is it possible they don't know where we're supposed to go from here?"

"We'll see," I answered solemnly. "If we wind up following them into quicksand or an alligator swamp, I guess then we'll know they didn't know."

We both sighed deeply and took off after the guys. We rode quite a distance along this road, which seemed to take us deep into the countryside and away from civilization. Finally the guys stopped and we stopped and after a short discussion it was decided that we would turn around and go back the other way. We were all sweating profusely when we arrived back at our starting point. We continued pedaling our bikes in the opposite direction from the way we had just come, and soon found ourselves riding into town, through a school zone, past an elementary school and into a neighborhood of neat little houses and fenced yards... well, most of the houses were fenced. The one unfenced yard we passed contained a huge dog, which appeared to be napping on the porch of a large rather dilapidated-looking house. Upon hearing our approach, he lifted his gigantic head and quickly spotted us. Immediately he sprang into action. He leaped off the porch and began barking viciously. He pounded across the lawn toward us. Marie and I both screamed and practically plowed over Jim and Stan in an effort to maneuver our bikes in between theirs.

"Everybody, stop and get off your bikes," Stan commanded, which we did. The dog was snapping and barking ferociously at all of us as we used our bicycles as shields to protect us from what looked to be very sharp, bared fangs. The dog lunged from one of us to another.

"Oh my gosh. He doesn't look very friendly," I cried. "What are we going to do?"

"I don't think this is the way to the park!" Marie responded, her voice rising.

Jim reached into his pocket and pulled out a long strip of beef jerky. When he spoke, his voice was calm and controlled.

"Hey there, boy. Come mere. Wanna chew on something? Come on, fella. How about a snack? Here, boy!"

He waved the jerky back and forth. The mongrel stopped snapping but maintained a low growl as he studied Jim. He jerked forward a few feet in Jim's direction and then jumped back. He repeated this action growling, lunging, and retreating several more times as Jim continued offering the jerky. Finally, the dog moved close enough to actually sniff the beef jerky being offered to him. Just as he was about to snatch it from Jim's hand, Jim yelled, "Fetch it boy," and with a snap of his wrist, he flicked the jerky away. Predictably, the dog turned and tore after the jerky and we used this distraction as our opportunity to take off like bats out of hell. By the time the dog retrieved the jerky and turned back to us, we were at the end of the street, flying around the corner and disappearing from sight. We pedaled through the neighborhood and continued along the road leading toward the shopping district. We stopped at a red light.

"So much for the coastal road route to the park," I mumbled to Marie.

"I guess we took the wrong road." Marie said to no one in particular.

"Hey!" Stan shouted. "Check it out. Isn't that the bike outfitter shop right over there?"

Sure enough, across the street and several store fronts over was the bike rental store where we'd picked up our bicycles earlier that morning for the coastal downhill ride.

"Well, this is even better!" Jim exclaimed. "We can drop off our bikes, grab a little lunch and head for the beach! Are you girls game?" We nodded mutely and followed our companions down the street to the bicycle outfitter store.

We dropped the bikes and other equipment off at the shop and left. As we rounded the corner and hurried toward a Hawaiian grill, we noticed it again. There was the big black town car which had nearly run us off the road near the top of Waimea Canyon.

"Hey! Isn't that the town car… ?" I began.

"That's the one," Stan interrupted. "Whoever's driving that thing is going to hear from me."

As we approached the driver of the town car, I happened to catch a movement out of the corner of my eye. I turned to see a familiar figure emerging from the Hawaiian grill carrying a takeout container. She was wearing a vibrant orange hat, huge sunglasses, a perfectly pressed blouse, linen slacks, and some famous guy's ridiculously overpriced shoes. It was none other than our old friend, Violet Katz!

"Violet!" I shrieked in surprise. "What are you doing here?"

By now everybody had turned away from the chauffer to stare at Violet. A big smile spread across her features, and she laughed with glee.

"I don't believe it! Can it be Kay Taylor and Marie Davies? Well, look at you! You went from sitting in a boring coffee shop in Pennsylvania, to this jewel of the Pacific! Look at the two of you... or is it now the *four* of you?"

Stan and Jim stood there with their mouths hanging open. Violet extended her hand to Stan.

"Hello there! I'm Violet Katz, and I have no idea which of these exotic creatures you are with, but I can vouch for both of them." She laughed warmly.

Stan, who was only inches taller than Violet, took her hand and shook it briefly. He nodded politely.

"I'm Stan Lawrence and this is Jim Rugger." Jim stepped forward and shook Violet's hand.

"It's a pleasure meeting you," Violet said. There was something so charismatic and charming about Violet, it was impossible to truly be upset with her over anything, and the last thing I felt at this moment was upset with Violet, but Stan plowed ahead.

"Is this your car?" Stan inquired, motioning toward the black town car.

"Why, yes it is… at least for the moment. I'm using it here while doing some geological studies. Why? Do you need a ride somewhere? I'd be happy to take you."

"No, thanks," Stan replied casually. "We have our own car just around the corner at the bicycle shop."

"Oh! Are you shopping for bicycles?" Violet's expression was one of confusion.

"No, actually we rented some bicycles earlier for a ride down the Waimea Canyon. You didn't happen to be driving up there earlier this morning were you?" Stan steadily held Violet's gaze.

"Why, yes, I was!" Violet smiled again. "I was up there this morning. Come to think of it, we passed some people on bicycles! That was *you?* Oh my gosh! Isn't that amazing?"

"Yeah, amazing," Jim murmured.

Stan continued, "Well, did you know your car almost ran over these exotic creatures you're so anxious to vouch for? Your driver honked his horn at them, which scared them out of their wits and caused them to crash on their bikes."

"No." Violet's head jerked toward her driver. "Jordan, did you honk at them?"

Her driver had stepped from the car and was standing at attention near the driver's door. He answered respectfully and honestly.

"Yes, Miss Katz. I did. There were several people on bicycles, but these two were riding dangerously close to the center line. I sounded the horn to warn them to move to the side for their own safety. I meant no harm. Sorry ladies."

His face colored slightly as he nodded in our direction. Marie immediately began walking toward him and started apologizing profusely. Jim grabbed her hand and pulled her back to where the rest of us were standing.

Violet turned back to us, shaking her head. "I'm sorry that happened. We were driving up Waimea Canyon this morning, but I was, unfortunately, on a conference call and not paying that much attention. I'm terribly sorry. Kay, Marie... how can I make this up to you?"

Suddenly, I felt miserable and upset with Stan for even mentioning the unfortunate episode. I paused for a moment and then heard myself say, "Don't worry about it, Violet. It's not like we were seriously injured or anything. We overcorrected and fell, that's all. We shouldn't have been out in the middle of the road like that. Your driver is right."

"Well, right or wrong, you were hurt and I feel terrible." She looked more carefully at me. There was no way I could hide the scrapes on my knees, wrists, and hands.

"Oh my heavens, Kay! You really are hurt!" Violet gently held my hands and looked more closely at the cuts and scrapes, which looked worse than they felt.

"Listen girls, I must do something for you. I must!" She paused, thinking. "I have an idea."

Suddenly Stan broke in, "Why don't you ladies talk? Jim and I will be inside getting some lunch." He leaned in and gave me an affectionate squeeze. Jim winked at Marie, and they turned and walked into the grill. Violet watched them go and then turned again to us.

"Okay girls, what's going on? What's the deal with these guys? Is it serious? Are you in *love?* I hope so, because it sure looks like they are!"

For a moment we just stood there without speaking. We had no idea if there was any kind of anything happening with Stan and Jim, serious or otherwise.

Marie finally spoke. "We met them on our first day here. Our hotel activity person talked us into playing beach volleyball, and they were our teammates."

Violet stared at Marie in amazement. "Volleyball? You? You're kidding, right?" She was shaking her head in disbelief.

"It's a long story, Violet," I interjected. "But to make it short, they're best friends and business partners, and Marie hit it off with Jim, and Stan and I... well, Marie and I thought we had something special with these guys, but they're leaving the island tonight in order to do a business deal tomorrow on Maui, and we're going home to Pennsylvania on Sunday, so we'll probably never see them again, and that's the end of the story."

"Really. Hmmm." Violet mused. "Well, we can certainly improve on *that* story!" A Cheshire cat sort of grin began to spread over her face. "Listen, girls! If your men are going to Maui, then so are you! I have a home on Maui! I'll make all the arrangements for you to come there this evening. I own a yacht, which is anchored just off of Kauai at the moment. It's at your disposal. How about it? Why not gather your luggage and cruise over to Maui tonight!

You can rest and recuperate at my house. We can spend a little time down on my private beach, and I can give you a tour of the island, whatever you like! But before we do any of that, we need to plan how you are going to surprise these two gorgeous men of yours who both appear to be smitten with you, if I do say so… and I do!" She laughed gaily. "Jordan will handle your travel needs, and my house staff will make you comfortable once you arrive. Will you come? Please? You really must!"

We hesitated for just a moment as we considered Violet's offer. It did sound like a perfectly perfect plan. We were unable to hide our excitement as we leaned in toward Violet conspiratorially.

"Are you sure, Violet?" Marie asked anxiously. "What about our rental car?"

"Oh, for heaven's sake! Give me the keys. Where is the car now? I'll have Jordan take care of it," Violet responded confidently. "I have a little work to do back on Maui before I see you, so I'll be flying over there within the hour, but I'll instruct Jordan to pick you up at your hotel and take you to the yacht later this afternoon, as soon as you're ready. Do you still have my card?" she asked.

"Right here," Marie pulled the still crisp business card from her fannypack.

"Good! Let me add Jordan's cell number on there. He'll be waiting for your call. Just contact him as soon as you're ready." She jotted the number on Marie's card. "And girls? Don't say anything to… " she gestured with a tilt of her head, "*them.* We're going to surprise those two!" She giggled uncharacteristically, and so did we. Just at that moment, Stan and Jim emerged from the grill balancing takeout containers and drinks in their arms. They set everything down on one of the small tables outside the grill. Jim hurried to Marie's side.

"Okay, what are you girls up to? What's so funny?"

Marie's face became serious before she responded, "That's for us to know and you to find out! Gosh, I haven't said that since I was ten." Then she burst out laughing. Violet and I joined in, while Stan and Jim looked on uncertainly.

Violet hugged Marie and I, whispering in our ears as she did so, "See you both soon!" Then she turned to leave, all business once again. "Well girls, as always, it's been a delightful pleasure running into you!" She nodded at the guys. "Nice meeting you, Mr. Lawrence… Mr. Rugger." The guys responded with hesitant smiles and a little wave goodbye. Jordan was courteously holding the door open for Violet as she walked toward him. She gracefully climbed into the car. We all smiled and waved as Jordan pulled away. It seemed we were finally going to get the kind of adventure we'd been waiting for.

Over lunch at the grill, we began asking the questions that needed to be asked—questions like, where were they staying in Maui, when were they flying out? What kind of business presentation were they planning and where would their presentation take place? To all our questions, Jim and Stan were forthcoming with all sorts of valuable information. After a while, they started asking us about *our* itinerary and when we would be going back to Pennsylvania. We were a little vague about our plans for the following day, and mostly talked about things we still needed to do before flying home on Sunday. We still had souvenirs to buy and then we were going to have to somehow locate the amazing, *supercalifragilistikexpialidocious* Mary Poppins herself, in order to discover how one fits an entire room full of stuff into a single carpet bag. We had little hope of jamming our mountain of clothes along with all our newly acquired purchases inside our traveling cases. Since it cost a pretty penny to get our luggage to Hawaii, it would cost an astronomical one to get them back home. We continued chatting as we drove back to the hotel.

Jim updated us as he drove. "We meet with the Kona corporation people in Maui tomorrow, but we have an appointment with Mr.Kamuela here in Kauai in a couple hours, so I guess we'll have to start thinking about getting over there pretty soon."

Jim looked at Stan and there was a moment of awkward silence as the car pulled into the hotel parking lot. I wondered how this good-bye scene would play out. Jim checked his watch.

"Would you two care to join us for a final walk along the beach?" He reached for Marie's hand. "How about it, Marie?"

"Shall we?" Stan touched my shoulder and ran his hand down my arm. The shiver of excitement, followed by a wave of relief, washed over me as I realized we were to have a little more time together. I noticed Marie visibly relax in her seat as she smiled at Jim. That was a big *yes.* We all strolled down to the beach. The four of us laughed and talked together as we walked barefoot through the lapping waves, but soon we began moving apart. Within minutes Jim and Marie were lagging a significant distance behind us. The light, easy banter of four people chatting informally became the private, serious talk of courting couples.

"I'd like to keep in touch with you, Kay, after we leave here."

"Me too," I replied.

"We could e-mail and call each other, I suppose. But I'd really like to have you come and spend some time with me in Arizona. I'd like you to meet my family and friends. Would you… consider coming to Arizona for a visit?"

"I guess that depends on the time of year," I replied carefully.

"Well, I think you should come next week," he responded lightly. "August really isn't *that* bad in Phoenix." Stan gave my hand a squeeze.

"Sure, Stan, not that bad if you're an iguana. Tell you what, why don't you come visit me in Pennsylvania during the summer, and I'll come visit you in Phoenix during the winter. That way we get the best of both worlds."

"That's a thought." Stan hesitated and then looked away. When he spoke, it was so softly I could hardly make out the words. "You know, Kay, we never slept together."

"Yeah, I think I would have remembered," I replied.

"No, that's not what I meant… well, you know what I meant. It's just… I haven't wanted another woman like this since Janice." Stan was visibly uncomfortable.

"What are you suggesting Stanley?" I looked innocently up into his face. An expression of distress immediately registered across his features. I continued looking steadfastly into his eyes. After a moment's reflection, his expression softened, and he looked thoughtful.

"Well, I'm sure getting tired of living alone. How about you?"

"A one week Hawaiian romance does not a marriage make. That's what I think, Stan. And I'm not doing *that* unless I'm married. It's my rule. You got yourself tangled up with a very old-fashioned girl this time, I'm afraid."

"That's exactly the kind of girl I want." Stan stopped and wrapped his arms around me. "If it's right, then it's right, Kay," he whispered into my ear. "I'd really like this to be right."

"Me too," I murmured as his mouth grazed mine. And then he was kissing me, passionately kissing me, my mouth, my ears, my forehead... my neck.

"Well, the sex thing is really more of a guideline," I whispered, arching my body into his.

"Me too." His voice was husky and deep. His mouth was sexy and sweet. "I think we make a pretty good fit. What do you think, Miss Taylor?"

"Mmmm, a perfect fit," I murmured as Stan pulled me closer.

"Hey guys, get a room," Jim shouted as he and Marie approached. We hurriedly pulled away from each other, laughing nervously.

"I was just testing something out with Kay," Stan called back to Jim.

"Testing for what, a career in the adult film industry?" Jim laughed hysterically at his own joke.

"No, moron. I was just trying to find out if Kay tasted like cotton candy, because that's what she smells like. Why? What does Marie taste like?"

"Marie? Hmm. She tastes just like soft... hot... delicious... sweet..." Jim was kissing his way up Marie's arm. When he was nearly to her shoulder and had a close-up view of her cleavage, he completed his thought. "Honeybuns," he finished. I rolled my eyes.

"Come on," I interjected. "Let's get back. You guys have a meeting, and Marie and I have some phone calls to make to our kids. Come on!" I grabbed Stan's hand, and we jogged along the beach back to the hotel. When we arrived, the guys walked us to our room.

"So, is this good-bye?" Stan asked.

"It needs to be... for now, anyway. You guys have to get to your meeting." I looked into Stan's amazing blue eyes, then quickly away as tears began to gather in mine.

"I'll see you soon, Kay," Stan whispered as he gave my hand a final squeeze.

"Okay," I replied with a little nod. We turned to Marie and Jim who appeared to be attached at the lips. "Embarrassing, isn't it?" Stan chuckled.

"Yeah, really disgusting. Some people have no self-control." I shook my head with a dramatic sigh.

"Okay, guys, save some for the wedding night." Stan tapped Jim on his shoulder. Jim, who appeared to be sucking Marie's face off, reluctantly stepped back.

"Bye, Marie. I'll be in touch." Jim gallantly kissed Marie's hand.

"Yes, I believe you will," Marie murmured with a secret little smile.

And then they were gone.

Once the door of our room was closed behind us, we started frantically pulling clothes off of hangers and out of drawers. It was truly a whirlwind packing experience. Within an hour we managed to organize all of our belongings and jam them into our travel bags. All that remained was to check out of the hotel and meet Jordan with the car. Marie made the call to his cell phone, and Jordan told us the car would be waiting outside the lobby in twenty minutes.

"Wow," I said as we surveyed our room for the last time. I grabbed Marie's hand. "What do you think Marie?"

"I think *now* we're having a real adventure!" she responded happily.

ANCHORS AWAY

Jordan was standing by the town car, looking very official in his polished black shoes and finely pressed uniform. He expertly loaded all our bags in the trunk and stacked the rest on the extra bench seat in the back, and then drove us to the pier where we boarded the most beautiful yacht we had ever seen. It was one of those dream yachts you see featured in nautical magazines. It smelled like wood soap and fresh, clean sheets just dried outside on a bright, breezy spring day. The sun was low in the sky when the ship's engines came on and the yacht eased out of the slip. Everything was calm and tranquil as the ship cut smoothly through the water. We leaned a little breathlessly against the rail watching the sunset. Once the sun was down and the breeze picked up, I told Marie I was going inside the cabin to find a sweater.

Shortly after I left Marie at the rail, there came the sound of a heavy splash not far from where Marie stood and a moment later, the voice of the watch called out those colorful words you only hear in movies, "Man overboard!" Except, this time it was for real. Then a second voice shouted, "What's going on? Is a man in the water? Get some light out here! Lower a lifeboat!"

Marie's brain went into overdrive. As luck would have it, there was a stack of folded deck chairs resting along the inner wall directly behind her. She rushed to secure one. Marie, who has an overactive imagination anyway, was now picturing herself on the bridge of the yacht with the captain. All the staff and passengers (including Violet, of course) were grouped admiringly on the deck below looking up at the sweet little ceremony in which the captain made a speech about Marie's presence of mind in an emergency and, by way of dramatic conclusion, pinned a medal of honor on her favorite patriotic red, white, and blue blazer.

The deck chair was heavy and awkward, but surely it would serve as a suitable floating device until help arrived. She managed to drag one to the rail, and as she hoisted it, the vision of everyone cheering and clapping while the captain awarded her that medal rushed into her mind. With herculean effort, she heaved the unwieldy object over the edge. Due to the darkness she could scarcely see what she was doing, but she heard.

There was a crack like the sound of a bat hitting a ball. Marie leaned over the railing and peered down. Searchlights flashed on from several locations all around the yacht. Suddenly, it was all too clear what had happened. The chair was wobbling about on the surface of the water, but there was no trace of the man. It appeared that, after failing on her first attempt to immobilize one man during the beach volleyball tournament earlier in the week, Marie had now succeeded in knocking another one unconscious on this, her second try. She had landed her missile squarely on the top of whoever it was's head. There was a lot of running on the part of the crew, staff, and other guests. A lifeboat was lowered, and everybody in the cabin rushed outside. Suddenly in the distance, a powerful motor roared to life and the form of a speedboat raced away into the night.

Somehow I suspected Marie of having some unfortunate connection with what had just transpired. I saw her standing back in the shadows, apart from the others, looking as if a deck chair had just fallen on her.

I went over to stand beside her and asked in a low voice, "Did you do that?" Marie managed a weak "yes," and I said, "Okay, we're now going to calmly walk away from here," as though we could just somehow walk off into another galaxy.

I grabbed her arm, and we walked in the opposite direction. I knew then how it felt to be harboring a fugitive from justice. Silently we walked around the deck, returned to the scene of the crime and, with expressions of innocent cherubs, asked what the commotion was all about. We were told that a professional thief, posing as a member of the staff, had just committed a robbery, stealing over a million dollars' worth of diamond jewelry from a safe in Violet's private quarters. He had escaped into the water and swam to a waiting speedboat, which was now miles away. It was a well-planned, perfectly executed heist. Unfortunately, one of Violet's most trusted employees had seen the man running from the scene of the crime. He chased the thief and jumped into the water after him, but some crazed member of the staff had hit him with a deck chair and sunk him. Steeling myself to hear the worst, I asked if he was dead. Marie couldn't speak. Momentarily, the word came that the man had been pulled from the water and would live. Marie decided she wouldn't feel right the rest of her life unless she gave herself up and told the captain she'd done it. We found our way to the bridge and bravely asked for the captain, who agreed to see us. There was no crowd below looking on with admiration for Marie's "medal of honor" ceremony, but the captain was extremely kind and commended her for making an effort to help, even though she wound up knocking the poor man unconscious. After the loyal employee had been hauled back on board, the doctor administered first aid, wrapped his head in a bandage, and announced he was going to be all right. Marie asked if she could see him and offer her condolences, and we were granted permission to go to the medic's cabin where we found none other than Violet's chauffer, Jordan, resting in bed with his head swathed in white bandages. His eyes were closed. Marie's mouth fell open, and she seemed to have lost her ability to speak. Evidently Jordan heard us because he opened his eyes.

"Are you okay, Jordan?" I asked meekly.

"I've been better, Miss Taylor, but they tell me I'll be shipshape soon enough. I got a gash on my head and a minor concussion, but what really gets me is that I didn't catch the low life who robbed Miss Katz. I saw him sneaking out of her room, and I could see her safe had been broken into, so I went after him. But he'd gone over the edge, and I didn't have time to call for help, so I just went in after him. The officer on duty saw me and raised the alarm. I almost had that lousy so and so too, when that chair landed on me."

"Oh," was all I could manage.

"We're sorry you got hurt, Jordan," Marie said in a tiny voice.

"I sure hope they catch the guy who robbed Miss Katz," Jordan continued. I knew there was something *off* about him. It was why I was watching him."

"Isn't there *something* we can do for you?" Marie implored. "Can we get you anything? Maybe some chicken soup or maybe something… stronger?"

"No, thanks, ladies. I'm being well cared for here. You go on and have a nice evening."

Marie didn't move. It was as though she was glued to the floor. Her lip quavered and her eyes began to tear up.

"Don't feel bad for me, Miss Davies. I'll be fine."

Marie continued to stand there. Finally she broke the silence.

"It was me, Jordan," she blurted out. "I'm the one who tried to kill you… I mean *save* you. I'm sorry you got hurt." She was sniffing loudly. I mutely handed her a Kleenex.

A smile began to spread across Jordan's face.

"Well, you're a good shot, Miss Davies. I'll give you that. Is this how you get back at me for honking at you on the road this morning?"

Marie looked miserable. "Of course not, Jordan! How can you *say* that!" She started sniffing louder.

"Oh, don't cry, Miss Davies. I was only joking. Now look, you ladies go on now. You don't want to miss any meals on this boat. The kitchen staff has an outstanding dinner menu. Order some champagne and raise a glass to me… and Miss Davies… it's okay."

He lifted his palms in supplication while nodding at her encouragingly. For a moment I thought Marie was going to throw herself at him and start kissing his hands or something but instead, she just faintly smiled, and we quietly backed out of the room.

We slowly walked back to the cabin where we were greeted as though nothing untoward had happened and were shown into the dining room. We sat down on comfortable captain's chairs at a beautiful mahogany table. We requested and were given iced goblets and bottles of Pellegrino sparkling water to drink. The first course was the soup course, which was a white cream soup with fat, soft dumplings and succulent chunks of lobster, fresh rolls with whipped butter, followed by a salad of baby greens, dressed with a delicious vinaigrette. Then came plates of tantalizing shrimp scampi and sweet tender scallops and steamed asparagus, and for finishing, a delicate puffed pastry filled with whipped, lemony, sweetened cream cheese and a raspberry reduction drizzled over and around the plate with several beautiful ripe berries scattered around the pastry. It was almost too pretty to eat… almost. Marie, in her distress, began the meal by hardly touching her soup, but by the time the main course arrived, she had begun to feel more herself and her appetite returned. After dinner we requested two glasses of champagne. Neither Marie nor I drank alcohol, but for Jordan we decided we must at least "raise a glass" as he had asked. The pretty drinks arrived and we lifted them in the air.

"To Jordan," I said soberly.

"To Jordan," Marie echoed.

We both took a sip. I started to cough. Marie dropped her glass as she gagged on the fiery liquid. "Why would anyone choose to drink something that tastes like cleaning fluid?" she choked.

We quickly grabbed our water goblets and gulped what was left of our water. Dinner was over. We stood and left the room. We made our way to what appeared to be the library with shelves of beautifully bound books. The room itself was very large and filled with inviting couches, easy chairs, lovely end tables, and softly lighted lamps everywhere. After perusing the ship's extensive library, we sat down in a couple plush rocking recliners with our book selections. We were served hot chocolate and cookies and covered with soft, fleece blankets. We were being pampered and indulged and loving every minute of it. We read, dozed, and discussed anything and everything, which is what Marie and I always did. Later, we were shown to our luxurious sleeping quarters and fell upon the sumptuous beds, still completely dressed, where we succumbed to the gentle lull of the ship's rocking.

Early the following morning the ship sailed into the quay of the Maui port. The moment the gangplank was down, four porters rushed on deck in the manner of a buccaneer boarding party, seized our luggage, and hustled it, and us, off the deck. Within moments, an agreeablelooking, uniformed man appeared. He smiled and introduced himself as our "new driver, Fritz." He instructed the porters hauling our luggage to "follow him." A sleek black limousine waited at the curb. Soon we were all loaded up and headed for a day filled with hopeful dreams and expectations.

DAY SIX: OUR ISLAND ADVENTURE CLIMAX

We were driven along a coastal road in Maui, although all the roads seem to be coastal when you're driving around an island. We began to notice that Maui was noticeably different in appearance from Kauii, which surprised us because we thought all the Hawaiian Islands would look exactly the same. The landscape wasn't as lush and, in fact, looked a little dry and drab along the hillsides. We asked Fritz about it, and he told us that we were on the "desert" side of the island, which didn't get as much rain. He assured us that this island had more variety than all the other Hawaiian Islands and we would soon be able to see it for ourselves.

We drove along for fifteen or twenty more minutes before departing the main road. Fritz turned off onto a narrower road banked on either side with immense trees, the uppermost branches meeting overhead, creating a sort of shady arbor. Masses of well-tended flowers and shrubbery led the way to a pair of massive black iron gates with leaping dolphins set in ovals in the center of each side. The gates opened in that *abracadabra* kind of magical way, and Fritz continued on to a large circular driveway, behind which rested a graceful manor straight out of *Gone with the Wind,* with wonderful white Corinthian columns lined up along the front portico. It was a mansion that screamed wealth and distinction.

So *this* was where Violet lived.

Fritz pulled up to the front of the house and as if on cue, two young men in khaki shorts, polo shirts, and jaunty caps burst through the front door and began hauling our luggage inside. Fritz opened our door, and we followed him to the entrance of the house. Upon entering the foyer, we heard Violet in the background giving instructions to the various domestics she employed, and then she sailed into the room, looking fresh, beautiful, and welcoming.

Suddenly, all Marie's pent-up emotions over Jordan and the deck chair she had flung overboard, spilled out. She collapsed into Violet's arms and howled over the awful thing she had done and how badly she felt. Wonderful, generous Violet was quick to dismiss the entire thing as an "accident anyone could make," and she went on to explain how the whole affair was just ridiculous because the jewels weren't even real. They were very good copies, but copies nonetheless.

"That man will be in for a big disappointment if he ever tries to fence *those* jewels," she expressed with a bitter little smile. Discussion over, she hurried us into breakfast.

We sat at a grand table near a large picture window. The sun sparkled off the ocean in the distance, and a lovely new day presented itself to our appreciative gaze. Violet told us this was where she, as a little girl, had spent her idyllic summers. Her house was up on a rise with wrap-around windows offering commanding views of the Pacific and surrounding hills, which were incredibly beautiful. The houses in the distance were pretty beach homes and helped create a most pleasant landscape. Marie went pseudo-literary and kept saying it was just like William Wordsworth's memories of Walden's Pond, which I thought rather affected of her. We spent an enjoyable hour eating and listening to Violet talk about the island. After breakfast we changed into our swimsuits, walked down to the beach, and ran in the surf (but not too strenuously). It was the first time during our week in Hawaii that we actually *cavorted* in the ocean. I did not count my regrettable experience snorkeling as *cavorting* in the ocean. Dressed in a flowered sundress and matching hat, Violet relaxed in a comfortable lounge chair under a colorful umbrella, looking very cosmopolitan and fine. After we had played, jogged, and splashed in the waves long enough, we trekked back to Violet's house, showered, and dressed in fresh clean clothes befitting Hawaiian tourists.

Once we were back downstairs, Violet ushered us into a lovely wood-paneled sitting room and suggested we pull up chairs and plan our strategy for surprising "the guys."

"I think we need the element of surprise," Violet began. "What do you girls think?"

We agreed enthusiastically, imagining the rapturous pleasure that would greet us when we magically appeared out of nowhere, surprising Stanley and Jim. Having made a point of securing the pertinent information the preceding day, we told Violet where the business meeting was being held, with whom, and the time.

"Hmmm," she mused. "Sounds like a lunch meeting. Since they are meeting at a large hotel, the meeting most likely will take place in the hotel restaurant. It is famous for its five star cuisine. People have business meetings there all the time. Lord knows I've had enough of them there. What do you say we all go out to lunch at a five star hotel restaurant today?" Violet called the hotel restaurant and checked on a reservation for a Mr. Kona. There was a Kona party scheduled for one o'clock. Violet then made a reservation for us at two o'clock. The plan was set.

"Time to begin your beauty preparations!" Violet announced.

Violet's bathroom vanity managed to look like a combination beauty shop and spa with professional styling chairs and equipment all over the place. Her garage-sized closet was like walking into the women's section of a department store.

She made a phone call and twenty minutes later, four professional beauticians appeared at her front door. They went to work on us, first our hair and makeup. Violet watched over the proceedings like a mother hen watching over her baby chicks. We began by having our faces covered in some creamy, white, grainy stuff. The effect was that of a couple women who had been bobbing for apples in wallpaper paste. Our heads were wrapped in towels, and we stretched out in her styling chairs while our faces were pelted with blasts of steam from some machine attached to Violet's wall. The only thing attached to my vanity wall was a medicine cabinet, filled with an assortment of old rusty razors, dried out deodorant bars, three tubes of partially used Preparation H, two manicure kits with nothing left inside but cuticle sticks, and several tubes of who knows what that ointment is which expired in April of 1984.

We sat in Violet's *spa* room being steam-spritzed for half an hour while our toenails and fingernails were expertly filed, buffed, and polished. After the masks came off our faces, we had our eyebrows tweezed and shaped, which was painful, but according to Violet, necessary. Our hair was colored, cut, and styled in chic, new looks. Our faces were made up to model-like perfection. Two and a half hours after beginning the whole process, Marie and I stood in front of a large mirror. I staggered back. We barely recognized ourselves. We were astonished by the two stunning women smiling back at us from the mirror. Our reflections looked glossy, fresh, and quite beautiful. Violet was even more thrilled than we were. She ushered us into her closet area where it became apparent that she was also going to dress us for this luncheon-surprise scenario. Marie and I glanced at each other doubtfully. We couldn't picture how this was going to work. Violet was quite a bit taller than we were and, even if we *could* fit into her pants, the legs would drag a mile on the floor, but Violet wasn't thinking pants. She started pulling out beautiful dress suits and colorful sun dresses. We tried on one after another until we had achieved a *look* that Violet thought "perfect." I ended up in some poofy-skirted designer frock that boosted my cleavage practically to my chin and cinched my waist to tininess I never imagined possible. Marie wound up in a pencil skirt and fitted jacket which made her look a little like movie starlet Bette Davis back in the day. Violet threw herself together in under twenty minutes, looking exotic and startlingly different in a long black wig. She looked as though it was she, and not us, who had spent hours primping.

We arrived at the restaurant fashionably late and stepped into the softly diffused lighting that cast a pinkish glow over the room. Immediately we all searched the room for Stan and Jim. They didn't appear to be there. Suddenly Violet grabbed my arm and indicated with a slight movement of her head a booth in the far corner of the room. Two familiar looking men were sitting with two very attractive women with whom they appeared to be deeply immersed in conversation. Marie and I glanced at each other in dismay. We began to turn around to leave, but Violet grabbed our arms and steered us into the room. We followed our waiter to a table by one of the windows, only yards away from where Jim and Stan were sitting. I stole a look over at their table. It was them. They both looked up as we made our way to the table. Neither of them showed any sign of recognition as we walked past, and they quickly turned back to their conversation with the two beautiful women sitting beside them. I pulled my elegant Louis XVI chair a little closer to our table and miraculously managed to place it in the one spot on that beautiful parquet floor where one of the chair legs sank into a small knot-hole. I sat down with a thud and went right over backwards like an intoxicated giraffe. Immediately, all eyes in our corner of the restaurant turned to me. My dress flew over my head, and I scrambled to pull it back down. I frantically looked over and noticed

Jim Rugger smiling in pure amusement. He still had not recognized me, but then I saw Stan. He was staring at me, wide-eyed, in pure disbelief. I quickly turned away. As I struggled to get my legs untangled, he stood up and walked directly over to me. He reached for my hand and pulled me firmly to my feet. My face was beet red, and I was afraid to look at him. This was not the surprise I had planned. Marie sat like a frozen statue, and Violet was watching the whole thing as though viewing a horror movie. I finally looked up at Stan, who had turned back to the woman with whom he'd been sitting and excused himself. In true Stanley-take-control fashion, he grasped my arm and guided me straight out of the restaurant, through the lobby, and outside the entrance. We sat down together on a small bench near the doors. Stan turned to look at me fully.

"If I didn't know any better, I'd swear you were Kay Elizabeth Taylor," he spoke quietly.

"We were going to surprise you," I responded glumly, looking away.

Ignoring my remark, Stan continued. "There's only one person I've ever seen take a fall like that, and it happened to a lady friend of mine at a luau a few days ago. You wouldn't happen to know who that lady friend was, would you?" he asked.

"Oh gee, Stan, I don't know. Could it be… oooh, now don't tell me, let me guess… wait a minute… let's see… who could it be… could it be… *meee?*" My voice sounded ominously shrill as I became increasingly infuriated over his questioning *me* while ignoring the glaring fact that he was obviously on a date with another woman.

Stan relaxed a little and smiled then, unaware of my rising anger.

"You know, you do seem to have a flair for dramatic mishaps. When I saw that beautiful, but strangely familiar looking woman tip over in her chair in the restaurant just now, well, imagine my surprise when I realized it was none other than the illusive Kay Taylor? So, what am I going to do with you, hmm?"

"Oh, I don't know, Stan. Maybe before you do anything with me, you need to get back to your *date* in there, and we can discuss it some other time... like never!" I angrily pulled my arm away, stood up, and began to walk away. His expression changed to one of enraged confusion.

"My date?" he countered defensively as he jumped to his feet and hurried after me. "What date? I don't have a date! That *woman* I was sitting with in there is a very successful distributor of Hawaiian women's wear here on the island of Maui. Jim and I are pitching our sportswear line to her and her assistant. Do you really think, after all we have been through together, that I would turn around and have some fling with another woman the very next day? Is that what you think of me?"

"Well I don't know, Stan," I responded angrily. "We don't know each other *that* well. I mean, how would *you* feel if *you* walked into this restaurant today and saw me sitting with some other guy?"

"I guess that would depend on what you did for a living, Kay!"

Suddenly I realized we were having our first fight. I stopped, and we both stared at each other. I thought about his heated response to my question and something about it struck me as very funny. I couldn't maintain my anger and felt it melt away. I started to giggle. Then Stan smiled, and the tension between us was broken.

"Actually, I can think of a couple interesting professions that might put me in a nice restaurant with some other attractive guy," I suggested.

"I can too, but I prefer not to," Stan replied. "I prefer to picture you in a nice restaurant with just me. Are you ready to go back in?"

I checked my hair and makeup and smoothed down my dress. I looked up at Stan who smiled and nodded his approval.

Arm in arm, we walked back inside.

Violet had commandeered the entire back corner of the restaurant. Tables were moved and people were re-arranged. The two young women who had been sitting with Jim and Stan were now sitting at our table, chatting and sipping champagne with Violet while Jim Rugger sat staring in stunned amazement at Marie, who appeared to be ignoring him. The manager of the restaurant hurried over to check my condition the moment I re-entered the restaurant. He apologized about the floor, assured me it would be immediately repaired, and informed me that my lunch "would be complimentary, of course."

Violet introduced us to Miss Lily and Miss Mia Kona, proprietors of Kona Hawaiian Women's Wear. After a pleasant visit, the two business women slid their laptops into briefcases which they snapped shut, and said their good-byes, with promises to fax signed paperwork to Stan and Jim's offices the following week. With warm parting smiles, they smoothly exited the restaurant.

Jim finally found his voice and waxed prosaic, quoting a bit of Lord Byron to Marie as he pulled his chair close to hers, "*She walks in beauty like the night… of cloudless climes and starry skies. And all that's best of dark and bright meet in her aspect and her eyes…*"

Marie blushed and batted her fake eyelashes.

"Oh no," I whispered to Stan. "He quotes poetry too? Marie does that all the time! We'll never hear the end of it!"

"Well, I've got some bad news," Stan whispered back. "I've been known to throw out a rhyme or two in my day… wanna hear one?"

"Oh no." I shook my head with a wry smile. "Well, if you must…"

"Okay. Here goes." He took my hand and looked heavenward for a moment, then he looked back at me with a confident smile. "Okay… here goes." He paused again.

"Yeah, you said that already…" More pausing and waiting… "Soo, you give up?"

"No! I'm thinking." He gave me a mock stern look. "Okay. Are you ready?"

I rolled my eyes. "Okay, shoot."

A final deep breath, and then he began.

"*There was a young lady named Kay, who joined in beach volleyball play. She hurried away but returned the next day to join Stan for a trip to Pompeii!* Pretty good, huh?" He leaned in close and whispered into my ear. "So Kay, what do you think? Wanna fly away with me to Pompeii?"

I gently disengaged myself and folded my arms. "Not bad for a limerick, but I'm not a big fan of visiting places filled with mummified human remains caused by a volcano that's still active. Hmm. I think I can do better than that."

I thought for a moment and then began.

"*There was a stud muffin named Stan, who had an ingenious plan. He saved his ladyee from a snake in the sea, then carried her off to Milan!*"

Stan's eyes widened.

"Wow! Does that mean you *would* fly away with me? I guess all that's left to do is book our flight to Italy!" Stan flashed me one of his mouthwatering smiles then suddenly pursed his lips as though in serious thought.

"*Stud muffin,* huh?" He took my hand and pressed it to his heart. "I don't know, Kay—saving my *ladyee*... I think that deserves a reward of some kind, don't you? How about giving me your hand?" he asked softly as he caressed my fingertips.

"I don't know. That's my left hand you're holding. Maybe it would be safer to give you my right one." I laughed a little nervously as I tried to pull my hand away, but he held it tightly.

"No, I like this one better," he replied. "But it looks like it's missing something."

I had removed my wedding band months ago, but the faint line indicating where it had been was still visible.

Oh no, I thought, panicking.

Stan continued unperturbed. "And, I think I have just the thing." He reached into his pocket and pulled out a small box.

My heart stopped and I felt anxiety grip my chest. I held my breath as he opened the box and presented it to me. Inside it, on a bed of gray satin, were five oddly shaped silver rings, all connected, but separate.

"What is this?" I asked.

"Something I was going to give you when you came to visit me in Phoenix, but you're here, so I think I'll just give it to you now."

I stared at the little clump of rings.

"You're kidding, right?" I picked up one of the rings and all the others came with it like a tiny, delicate chain. I tried to see how the rings were attached.

"It's a puzzle ring, Kay." Stan stated. "You have to figure out how to put it together." He watched me expectantly. I pressed all the rings together squeezing and rotating them, but they just fell back apart. I twisted and turned and tried to manipulate the five bands, but I could not make them fit together into one ring.

"This is hard," I said simply.

"That's what's so great about figuring it out," Stan replied. "After you get it put together into one ring, you can read the message on the inside."

"And the message is good for ten years, right? Because that's how long it will take me to put this Humpty Dumpty back together again." I placed the rings back in the box and dropped it into my bag. "Well, it will give me something to do on the plane ride home anyway. Thank you, Stan. Honestly... I'm not sure, but I think I love it."

As I leaned in to kiss his cheek, he whispered into my ear, "It was something you said."

I pulled back and looked up at him quizzically.

"Something I said?"

"Umm hmm," he replied, nodding. That was all he would tell me. We turned back to the others.

We ordered a huge macadamia nut brownie with lots of vanilla ice cream and hot fudge, which we all shared. Violet acquired more information about Stan and Jim in one hour than either Marie or I had obtained in a week. She was vivacious, generous, and engaging. She managed to make everyone around her feel important and interesting. As our plates were being cleared away, she invited Jim and Stan to join us for the remainder of the day, but since they hadn't anticipated seeing us again, they had booked late afternoon flights home and had to leave for the airport.

We said our good-byes outside the restaurant, which were a little more restrained this time with Violet standing there, but filled with promises of phone calls, e-mails, and a happy reunion sometime… soon.

The moment they drove away, Violet asked for a look at the puzzle ring Stan had given me. Evidently, Violet knew puzzle rings.

"I've always had a fascination for these rings," she said as she studied the bands. "Wow. This isn't your normal flea market puzzle ring, Kay. This is platinum. He must have had this specially made for you, but the pattern of the ring is common enough."

In thirty seconds she had amazingly fitted all the bands together and handed the ring back to me. Marie and Violet stood together watching me expectantly. I held it up to the light. Inside was an inscription which read simply, *Stan & Kay, a perfect fit.* I showed my two friends the tiny message.

"Mmmm, mmmm," Violet responded with a slight raising of her eyebrows and a shake of her head.

"It looks like he's got plans for you," Marie mused.

"Yup... looks that way," I replied. A slow smile spread over my face as I slipped the ring on my finger. "I guess we'll see. And, what about you?" I gave my best friend a light shove. "How do you like the name Marie *Rugger?*"

"Oh... I don't know. I suppose I could get used to it." Marie turned to us with her favorite Cheshire cat grin.

The moment was over. Not one for wasting time, Violet shepherded us to her car and drove us along something called the "Road to Hana" which, although beautiful, made Marie and I both nauseous because of the excessive twists and turns along the way. Then she took us to see the Haleakala volcano. The views of island and ocean from there were breathtaking. This was Violet's "island," and she loved every bit of it.

Although Marie and I enjoyed seeing Maui with Violet, our hearts were still back on the island of Kauai. Our best vacation memories were there and we knew that Kauai would be the island to which we would return... if we ever returned. And sitting together on the plane the following morning as we waved a final goodbye to Violet, we knew we'd be back one day. After all, Hawaii was a very popular *honeymoon* destination.